SIGH FOR A
STRANGE LAND

ALSO AVAILABLE FROM OPEN SPACE BOOKS

Where Lay My Homeward Path (Selected Short Stories of Edward Thomas)

The Cyclist in the Canal (e-book, short story)

www.openspacebooks.co.uk

SIGH FOR A
STRANGE LAND

MONICA STIRLING
WITH AN INTRODUCTION BY IRFAN SHAH

Open Space Books

First published in 1958 by Victor Gollancz

Printed and bound in Great Britain by Clays Ltd, Elcograf
S. p. A.

This edition of *Sigh For A Strange Land* published in 2023
by Open Space Books.

ISBN: 978-1-8384667-5-6

ACKNOWLEDGEMENTS FOR THE 2023 EDITION

We would like to thank the following people for their support with this project:

Brad Bigelow, wrote about *Sigh For A Strange Land* on his website, The Neglected Books Page, and noted the topical nature of the work, which in turn sparked the idea for this project.

Scott Thompson had already discovered the work of Monica Stirling and had written about it in his blog Furrowed Middlebrow. Scott was invaluable in helping me to trace Monica's family.

John Stirling is Monica's nephew and was supportive of the project from the start. John, it should be said, has his own book - *Never Work With Children or Animals* - which describes his years as a child actor up to his work running a donkey sanctuary.

Vickie Le Saché is Monica's niece. Not only was she incredibly supportive of this project, but the slivers of recollection she provided of her aunt have made a valuable contribution to the project.

To find out more about how this book will be raising funds for Ukraine, please go to our website at www.openspacebooks.co.uk

INTRODUCTION

So much for 'never again.'

When Russian military forces poured across large swathes of Ukraine in February 2022, streams of Ukrainians, seeking safety for themselves and their loved ones, scattered across Europe and the rest of the world. They became refugees, as so many others have become from places as far apart as Syria, Yemen and Afghanistan (and indeed from the East of Ukraine since 2014).

Monica Stirling's novel, *Sigh For A Strange Land*, was first published in 1958 and had been inspired by the Hungarian Revolution of 1956, in which around a quarter of a million civilians were displaced. In the novel, Resi, an adolescent in the care of her flamboyant aunt, is forced to flee her home when a violent uprising takes place. The land from which they escape is never mentioned explicitly which means that Resi, Aunt Natasha and Natasha's beloved companion Boris, are simply refugees from a nameless East European country. As such, and while remaining fiercely and gloriously individual, they lend themselves as archetypes; embodiments of the hope and hoplessness of exile.

This edition of *Sigh For A Strange Land* has been produced with the intention of raising funds to help those suffering from the invasion of Ukraine. The people there are asking, simply, to not be subjugated, to not be murdered – in fact, through their countless acts of courage, they are positively insisting on it. We felt we might do a little to help.

This book has been put together quickly and with the best of intentions. Two versions of the story were already in existence, and so a brief word on the text in this edition is probably in order: the novel first published in 1958 was immediately recognised for its charm. Acclaim certainly came its way, but it was perhaps a little muted. A far more concise version of the story appeared in three parts in the pages of the Atlantic Monthly the following year. In some ways, the story benefited from this stripped down telling, but in other ways, something of its colour was lost. For this edition, we have found a third way through the story, opting for the shorter version whenever brevity and flow were felt to be required, but remaining loyal to the more expansive text whenever possible. The result is the book you have now.

Finally, a few words on Monica Stirling, and only a few, because there is not a great deal of information readily available at present, although we hope that this book will serve as encouragement to rediscover her life and work. From the Atlantic Monthly and various potted biographies on the flyleaves of her novels we are told the following: that her parents founded and ran the

English Players theatre group in France between the two world wars and that Monica subsequently spent ten years of her childhood in Paris; that in the early years of the Second World War, she worked for the Free French at the De Gaulle headquarters in London, and that in 1942 she started writing. She became war correspondent for the Atlantic Monthly and returned to France after the Normandy invasion, where she wrote reports, and a number of short stories which won her a Metro-Goldwyn-Mayer award for a year's writing in Italy. Her first novel, *Lovers Aren't Company* was published in 1949 and was followed by a range of books from more novels to biographies of Ouida, Luchino Visconti, Letizia Ramolino Bonaparte and Hans Christian Andersen. She also wrote at least two books for children, *The Little Ballet Dancer*, and the magical *The Cat From Nowhere*.

From her niece, Vickie LeSaché, we are told something more personal - that she was adored by both Vickie and her brother, John, and that Monica nurtured Vickie's love of reading by sending her 'wonderful books.'

"My aunt was an amazing woman. She lived in a hotel in Lausanne and wrote everything in pencil - I still keep her box of many, many sharpened pencils!"

Monica never married. The proposals she did receive amused her, and the last relationship of which her family was aware was with French literary critic, Odette Arnaud. Monica was also popular - she could be an amusing, light-hearted companion - and counted among her friends such luminaries as Noël Coward,

Truman Capote and the French author, Colette. However, there were moments of shadow, too. Her nephew, John Stirling, has written that she never fully recovered from her experiences of accompanying American forces in the liberation of the concentration camps. Vickie adds that "I remember her speaking of her trauma at seeing, I think it was, the camp at Belsen, [John thinks perhaps it was Buchenwald] when they opened it for the first time after the war ended." Another friend, Oriel Malet, wrote that "this pain was threaded through her novels like a dark ribbon."

The trauma may have been one of the contributing factors to Stirling's suicide in Switzerland on 15th November 1983.

Monica Stirling's life, despite its end, seems to have been a fabulous one. The family is sure that she would have approved of the use to which *Sigh For A Strange Land* is now being put, and that in fact, she may yet be celebrating it.

Publishing Monica's book is an act of re-discovery, and a giving of voice to the refugee experience. It is a way of remembering these people, these stories, these wind-blown seeds - for Resi is, as we speak, crossing borders in Uzhhorod, Al-Wadiah, Rafar, Calais.

To Countess Marie Orlov *née* Kamichansky

PART ONE

'To sleep as snug as in the grave
In your kind bed, and shun the wave,
Nor ever sigh for a strange land
And songs no heart can understand.'
EDITH SITWELL, *The Sleeping Beauty*

CHAPTER ONE

The day the revolution started my Aunt Natasha was drunk. Not that I realized this at first. She'd gone to a name-day party the previous evening, and I hadn't heard her come in. But there was nothing unusual about this. Aunt Natasha is very dignified when drunk, and therefore quiet. She is also dignified when sober. I love Aunt Natasha. She adopted me after the death of my parents, whom I can't remember, although no one would have blamed her had she shifted the responsibility. My other blood relative, Uncle Matthias, cans caviar for exportation and owns a television set; but he was determined not to own me.

Aunt Natasha is not young, and her husband, the general, died before the war. I can't remember him; nor, I sometimes think, can she. Unless he was a very odd general: gentleness, according to her, was his dominant characteristic. Almost aggressively gentle herself, Aunt Natasha had lately taken to vegetarianism — although we made an exception whenever Uncle Matthias sent us caviar, which he didn't do often, luckily for Aunt Natasha's principles. Because she never cheated, maintaining that to say "fishes' eggs don't count" would be adding hypocrisy to wrongdoing, the thought of which made her scatter hairpins.

These hairpins often served as barometers. For example, when strewn over the floor of her room in the morning, they indicated that Aunt Natasha had been drunk the night before. We never discussed this, not because the matter embarrassed her, but because it didn't, so there was nothing to discuss. It was behaviour of this kind that made Uncle Matthias say Aunt Natasha was merely a child in his I-am-a-man-of-the-world-and-you-can't-fool-me voice. But he isn't and you can. He meant that despite hairpins he considered Aunt Natasha fundamentally simple and good. But having recently been a child myself, I know that children are not necessarily either simple or good.

This morning was a school holiday, but I got up at the usual time because I'd made a date to have my first permanent wave at eight o'clock, and the hairdresser lived way over on the other side of town. I'd been saving my chess winnings for this permanent. In several contemporary novels recommended by the library committee the heroines' natural hair and freedom from cosmetics are particularly admired by the heroes. Here I think the authors are deviating from the truth—except when they prevaricate by making the natural hair consist of rebellious curls. Anyway, mine being rebelliously straight, I was longing for this permanent. Longing makes me hungry, so I hurried out of bed and across the room to the tin safe where we keep food.

In it were a bowl of bean soup, half a baked potato, and some stale *hornashen*. I put half the soup in a saucepan, but the gas was so low the soup was barely tepid when I wanted it. Eating half the half potato, I daydreamed of other kinds of food. My desk-mate, Elsa, whose father is a porter at the American Embassy, once gave me a magazine full of big, coloured advertisements: hamburgers, hot dogs, avocado pears, waffles with maple syrup, lemon meringue pie, and steaks bigger than my hand. Most of all I should have liked to try a layer cake that looked as snow does at the pole just after penguins have hobbled across it. Meanwhile I ate the potato slowly, so as to make it last. It was somewhat moldy, but I enjoyed the burned part.

While eating I stood beside the dressmaking dummy and looked out the window. It is mainly because some of Boris' jobs with horses have enabled him to win friends and influence people in one or two government offices that Aunt Natasha can carry on private dressmaking without being molested. In general, former property owners can operate only on sufferance; and in the case of shopkeepers it's not long before they're accused of sabotage. At this time of the morning there was usually a procession of people going by to work. They would hurry along in dark clothes, few ever looking right or left, their movements staccato as those of extras in the early Charlie Chaplin films shown at the Cinema Museum. But this morning the street was empty, except for a cat. It advanced prudently, stopping now and again to examine the gutter. Once it jumped on a leaf. It was an orange cat. Wondering uninterestedly where everyone had gone, I finished dressing. I didn't wash as, the tap being in Aunt Natasha's room, this would have meant disturbing her. There is a shower on the landing, but seldom any water, and never any hot water except when the janitor's wife wants to take a bath, a rare event.

As I was about to leave I suddenly remembered that Elsa had given me a glass tube of Alka Seltzer tablets in exchange for my doing her French translation. Her father had picked them out of an embassy trash basket, a place in which he often found objects of interest. Aunt Natasha had appreciated the last lot, so would be glad to see these. I managed to turn the handle soundlessly, and was about to tiptoe in when I saw that her bed was empty.

Fear broke out over me like sweat. Worrying as she did over me — in case I might be run over, for example, although there is very little traffic to be run over by — Aunt Natasha rightly assumed I worried over her, and she never slept away from home without warning me, even at curfew periods. My hand sticking to the door knob, I guessed at friends she might have felt like visiting after the party: old Nina, who is a masseuse but has no telephone and lives on the other side of town, between the Powder Tower and the deserted canal; Olga, who is officially a bad typist and unofficially an excellent fortune teller; Boris, who is Aunt Natasha's oldest friend and now trains circus horses — and at this point there was a loud hammering on the front door. The bell had been out of order for several months, and the electrician's waiting list was longer than a bus queue on a wet night. If nagged, the electrician would fly into a rage and announce he had only one pair of hands. Sometimes he even accused the impatient of being bourgeois.

"Coming," I shouted, thinking with relief that Aunt

Natasha had merely lost her key, "coming, darling," then I stopped. Outside stood not Aunt Natasha, but a policeman. I felt as if there were a large cold stone in my stomach. But I tried to look pleasant. They can make trouble, not theoretically but in practice, if one doesn't. After giving me a disapproving stare, he asked, in that smoothly dire voice that so often goes with a uniform, did Aunt Natasha live here? Yes, I said, swallowing "of course" just in time. Oh, he said, sneerily, then I'd better know she was at the Racnik hospital, having been taken ill in a public thoroughfare. The stone pressed deeper into my stomach, but I just managed to control myself. If one shows distress they are apt to think one has reprehensible motives for this. Which is often the case, from their viewpoint. Instead of trying "My aunt is inclined to be delicate," which might have led to their sending her to a Home, I said, "Thanks very much, I'll come right away." Then something odd happened. The policeman smiled sympathetically, so I smiled back, and for a few seconds it was as if there were no uniform making a third person in the doorway.

When I got to the end of the street, I realized I hadn't asked the policeman the Racnik's address. But he'd bicycled out of sight, so I turned back and across the big square to the post office. At this hour the square usually belongs to the men in dark blue, with peaked caps, who sweep up the leaves. Children on their way to school often annoy the men by shuffling their feet in the piled-up leaves, and when the sweepers brandish their brooms, the twigs make angry crackling sounds. But today no

19

one was touching the leaves, which lay where they had fallen, in heaps almost as bright as the orange cat. There was a faint smell of burning.

To my surprise, the post office was closed. There was no one outside but a speckled cat, caressing itself against a grating, and when I looked back across the square the only living creature in sight was another cat. Not for the first time I wondered why animals don't attack us. Suppose they suddenly realised how many of them there are, suddenly objected to being kept in fields, stables, byres, yards, zoos, reservations, being kept on duty. But I suppose they aren't organised for self-defence. Neither, in some respects, is Aunt Natasha. Another surprising fact was that there was no queue outside the bookstore, though there had been one all day yesterday, owing to the arrival of copies of two French books, *Cyrano de Bergerac* and a novel by Gilbert Cesbron.

Behind the post office I ran into one of the sweepers, his peaked cap on backwards. When I asked the way to the Racnik he looked annoyed and turned his back. When I tried to insist, he shooed me off with his broom. Next, I tried the baker's. The baker was outside, pulling down the iron shutters. All he would say, out of the side of his mouth, was "You don't want to go there now." On the railway embankment three children were playing marbles with pebbles. They'd never heard of the Racnik. In front of the closed gymnasium some young men in raincoats were running, their elbows close to their sides, their knees high. A small boy held the side door of the church of the Knights of the Cross open so that a man wearing a crash helmet could wheel his motorcycle inside. Far down the arcaded street that leads to tall old houses with high-pitched gabled roofs, there was a small detonation. Today, looking back on all this, I realize nothing was quite as usual that morning; but at the time I was thinking only of Aunt Natasha. Sometimes, when one is called to the hospital, there has been an accident.

I crossed the river — dark-green as magnolia leaves this morning, with here and there coffee-coloured streaks of alluvial mud — by the bridge of statues. The wind was tugging frantically at the flag over the castle. At the end of February 11th Avenue, there was a smell of gasoline. It came from a straggling crowd of people carrying jugs and making for the war memorial. This consists mainly of an old tank the colour of dried mustard, and it is only time that has transformed it into a memorial. Tanks fill me with terror. Bombs and bullets can kill unexpectedly, quickly, almost painlessly; but no one could see a tank coming nearer and nearer without knowing what to expect. After seeing that old film about the siege of Berlin, I used to have nightmares in which I was slowly chased by an army of giant tortoises, their soft heads gently swaying outside their hard shells, their necks looking like crumpled wrapping paper.

Running from the crowd, I found myself in a street I didn't know, long and straight, lined with small trees looking naked and isolated as town trees do when just planted. There was no one in sight until two dogs appeared. At the end of the street stood a grey statue of a liberator, speckled white by pigeons' droppings. An old woman was sitting on the steps at the liberator's feet, mending the cane seat of a chair. She had no front teeth and smelled of garlic. When I asked her the way to the Racnik she made growling noises, and the dogs came nearer and stared, as if amazed to hear a human using their language. I just managed to make out that I'd better be careful, it was one thing to get in but quite another to get out, they're devils in them hospitals, also that the Racnik was second on the left from the Victory Arch. I've forgotten who was victorious there, but many people were killed and some of their names are carved on the arch. Whenever we are advised to think of posterity, it strikes me that we are someone's posterity. This is not altogether an encouraging thought.

Beyond the arch people were running to and fro, shouting. I try to acquire courage but doubt I ever shall. Shouts, waving arms, and people gnashing as if their teeth were secret weapons make me tremble. I was beginning to fear I would never find the hospital when there it was, just past the statue of a reformer who was burned several hundreds of years ago: a big handsome building with windows, some of them paneless, surmounted by fragments of carved coats of arms. Immediately inside was a desk marked "Inquiries." A man in a greyish overall said Aunt Natasha certainly wasn't there, speaking as if my suggesting she might be were an insult. But another man, who was filling in forms, suddenly looked over his spectacles and said oh yes she was, on the second floor. He even accompanied me to the elevator, which had a placard on it saying "Temporarily out of order." In our apartment block the elevator wore a similar placard for eighteen months, after which Aunt Natasha stole it. She said the information had grown stale, not to say monotonous. Sometimes, when just a little drunk, she used to hang this placard round her neck.

The hospital stairs were painted a mustard colour like that of the memorial tank. I tried unsuccessfully to imagine anyone's going into a paint store and exclaiming, "Ah, that's just the colour I'd like." There were smells of anaesthetics, frying, and lavatories. The first ward I entered contained about twenty beds, close together, in each an old woman with tangled grey or white hair, and several front teeth missing. Looking at the hairs, each distinct as twisted wire, strewn over the battered scalps, I thought of the last ballet Aunt Natasha and I went to — and of how lucky Juliet was to die young, beautiful, and still expecting something from life.

Aunt Natasha wasn't there, so I ran out, and into a nurse with a dirty apron, who said she'd never heard of Aunt Natasha, and I'd no business wandering around as if I owned the place, whatever next, the thin end of the wedge. So I said placatingly that I was just going, and went down the passage and hid behind a wardrobe until she was out of sight. The second ward contained the same kind of old women as the first, inanimate as objects washed up after a storm, except for an occasional flicker in their eyes, such as one sees in the eyes of animals behind bars. Immediately I entered the third

23

ward, a hand rose from the furthest bed, and with it a faint but jaunty cry. So relieved that I was almost prepared to scold, I ran and clutched Aunt Natasha. All her hairpins were gone, and her soft moth-coloured hair floated round her shoulders, giving her the look of an elderly actress miscast as Desdemona.

"Look, Resi darling," she pointed at her black eye, "wouldn't you know I'd go and fall on my face. You'll have to conceal me, in the unlikely event of Matthias calling." She gave a deep infectious laugh. Uncle Matthias is not related to Aunt Natasha by blood, only by law, and distantly.

"How . . ." Then I stopped. In such circumstances, Aunt Natasha never remembers recent happenings. "What about coming home?"

"An excellent idea. So good of you to come, my darling. They were being quite tiresome about letting me out. Forms," she waved her long beautiful grubby hands, "filling in f-o-r-m-s, the great twentieth-century vocation. You'd think that . . ." Suddenly bored by this topic, she turned to the bed nearest hers. "Mrs. Wieder has kindly suggested that her husband might be able to do us a favor now and again. He's a butcher, and devoted to the circus."

This was the first I'd heard of our vegetarian period being over, and I looked with interest at Mrs. Wieder, who was mumbling what sounded like an apology.

"By all means," said Aunt Natasha graciously and, as if she'd been waiting for this signal, Mrs. Wieder popped a set of large false teeth into her mouth. They didn't altogether improve her appearance, but they did alter it. "You're very welcome," she said, distinctly, and she bowed, in as far as one can bow lying in bed. Aunt Natasha bowed back, on the same lines, but with different effect. The difference between Aunt Natasha and Mrs. Wieder was like that between bombed baroque and a prefabricated house that has collapsed because it wasn't put together properly in the first place.

Getting drunk must give pleasure or so many people wouldn't do it. In Aunt Natasha's case I think it reminds her of when she was young and beautiful, since at that time many of her friends drank a lot. It was part of the way they lived, like keeping tame bears, going to hear gypsies sing, having the kind of love affairs that go with tiaras, and never getting up from the table feeling one could immediately eat as much again. Yet she did not exactly regret that life, having thought it wrong even when living it. As a young bride, an admirer of Peter Stolypin, she assembled all the peasants on her country estate and announced she meant to share her land with them. She was amazed when they replied they needed time to consider her offer, and very hurt when they refused it on the grounds that she wouldn't be giving property away if there weren't something wrong with it. But although Aunt Natasha disapproved of that old life, it had left traces in her, like creases in a piece of cloth that only a hot iron can smooth out — and, now and again, one of these traces would get us into worse trouble than we were in at the Racnik.

When at last I found the nurse in charge of releasing

patients, she grumbled and thrust a handful of printed forms at me. I have known many shortages, but never one of forms. Aunt Natasha won't use them for lavatory paper, she says one must draw the line somewhere, and that in any case they would be just as nefarious in this capacity as in that for which they were intended. On the forms in question Aunt Natasha was required to certify that all her personal belongings had been returned to her in good and due form. In fact they were returned in a sackcloth bag with a list pinned to it: "one beret, one coat, one skirt (torn), one pair of boots, one purse (empty), one glove (left hand), one key, one packet of cigarettes (squashed)."

Greeting these elatedly, Aunt Natasha climbed out of bed. With her hair drifting over the shoulders of the grubby white cotton hospital nightshirt that stuck out around her legs, thin as a flamingo's, in their wrinkled pinkish-beige stockings, she looked more than ever like a miscast actress. One of her stockings was torn. I knotted my handkerchief, to remind me to buy thread.

Before leaving, Aunt Natasha bowed enthusiastically to so many people that I was afraid we were in for a busy week socially. She likes few things better than having our two rooms crammed with people all talking at the tops of their voices, while she adds cabbage to the pot of slowly cooking soup. At school we're often told to remember that older people find it hard to adjust themselves to modern life, but Aunt Natasha is in many respects better adjusted to it than I am. The facts of life don't shock her.

When at last we got away into the street, I saw that, for all her buoyancy, Aunt Natasha wasn't feeling her best. For one thing, she made a fuss about lacking an umbrella, insisting she'd had one on arrival, therefore the hospital must have stolen it. She became very agitated, connecting this imaginary theft with some of the executions she saw during the last war. The lampposts to which these particular people were strung are just around the corner from us. Her black eye was more apparent now than it had been indoors, and her hastily rolled-up hair made bulges in her dusty old beret.

Luckily there was no one about except a scurrying hunchback at whom Aunt Natasha looked longingly. Although she disapproved theoretically of superstition, she liked to touch a hunchback's hump but was too considerate to do so except in a crowded streetcar, where no one noticed. Similarly, she disliked seeing people break up the still burning remains of kindling sticks with a poker, thus sending their dead relatives to hell. When taxed with this, she would deny it, adding that in the first place the relatives were probably in hell anyway, and in the second that hell didn't exist. Then she would go right on touching humps, restraining pokers and, when very slightly drunk, tossing glasses over her left shoulder. Luckily, most of our glasses were in fact plastic cups.

We waited for about fifteen minutes, and still no streetcar came. The wind tugged at our clothes and made our teeth chatter. Somewhere in an upper room a radio was turned on. A large voice orated angrily, then was interrupted by a passage from *The Bartered Bride*. When this stopped abruptly, there was silence except for the wind.

"We really must get our radio mended," said Aunt Natasha apologetically.

"We will." But I knew we couldn't afford to just now. Suddenly exhausted by the thought of all we couldn't afford, I said: "Look, it's cold, and we're tired, so let's try and find a taxi in Government Square, and then" — I put my hand in my pocket and made sure the money was there — "then let's stop at the delicatessen downstairs and get some salami." Aunt Natasha had loved salami before vegetarianism set in.

"Do you think we could manage a bottle of beer, too?" She tried to make the question sound casual.

"I guess so." I touched the coins again.

"I could do with a glass of beer."

The way she spoke brought tears to my eyes, partly because it was she, partly because certain kinds of small greediness seem to me beautiful: on the side of life.

"Of course," I said warmly, "of course. You shall have —" and it was then that the tank came down the street.

As it crashed along, wobbling slightly, like the giant tortoises in my nightmare, Aunt Natasha pulled me behind a lamppost. I don't know what good we thought a lamppost would do us. There was a man standing up in the middle of the tank, only his head and shoulders visible above the manhole, and on his face a ferociously constipated look. I made my stare respectful enough for two — one cannot look respectful with a black eye

— and at last the tank turned a corner.

At the crossroads, between the remains of the synagogue burned by the Germans and the Roman Catholic Church shelled by the Russians, we saw a young man with a camera running as if pursued. He was going so fast that when he suddenly stopped we both jumped. He stood as if hypnotized, just across the street from us. We could see he was unusually handsome, and looked friendly. Suddenly he raised his arms, slowly and gracefully and purposefully, like a conductor during slow music. A dreamy smile spread over his face, and the camera hanging around his neck swayed like a pendulum. Moving nearer, we saw a surprised look come into his eyes, which were light grey and very clear. His arms were still uplifted when, all at once, he crumpled and fell.

Kneeling beside him, I turned to Aunt Natasha. Her face had a greenish tinge. Closing his eyes, she said, "Even the young may be glad to rest."

I nodded. But the idea that he would never open them again was so disturbing that I began to cry. One hand on his shoulder, one arm round me, Aunt Natasha looked hesitantly around the crossroads, empty except for the three of us, and said, "Something unusual's happening, don't you think?" A press card in the young man's pocket showed him to have been a foreign journalist, aged twenty-five. Underneath him a bloodstain spread, like ink in blotting paper. Distant rat-tattat sounds came nearer.

"Better go through the park," I said. Riots usually

took place near the shoe factories or university, at the other end of town. Aunt Natasha took my hand. Like hers it was clammy. From the corner we looked back at the young man, lying as if asleep, alone with his camera. Suddenly half a dozen men in raincoats jumped out of a doorway and ran past us, yelling. We couldn't hear what they said, but their tone made us run too. They were carrying machine guns. As we ran, I prayed that the delicatessen would be open. Aunt Natasha looked ill, and I knew she'd not eaten in the hospital, because whenever one of us eats out she saves a bit for the other.

The park gates were shut, but not locked. No one loitered beside the lake except a few ducks, their head inquisitively cocked at a metal chair overturned by the water's edge. When we came to the bandstand Two men wearing armlets were carrying a loaded stretcher up the bandstand steps, while a girl with her hair tied up in a yellow scarf tossed music stands over the balustrade. As the metal landed on the grass it made small thudding sounds. We did not talk much. Once Aunt Natasha said, "It'll be all right" for my benefit, and I said, "I'm sure it will" for hers.

On the other side of the park most of the streets were empty. Our footsteps sounded abnormally loud, and a sensation of being followed made us break into a run every now and again. Once we were brought up short by small clashes overhead and, looking up, saw a woman frantically closing shutters. We realized then that many of the houses we'd passed had had drawn shutters, although it was not yet midmorning. When we reached the post office square, we saw why the nearby streets were empty. It was seething with people, some of them tugging at the grille over the post office door and yelling. Among these I recognised a little man we were constantly seeing on the stairs – when he would scurry by with an unpleasant smile; or talking with the janitor in a doorway – when he would immediately break off the conversation and look at us as if he knew something about us we didn't know ourselves. He always wore a beret and carried a briefcase, and I had an irrational dislike of him – so much so that his presence here frightened me more than all the rest of the scene, through which violence was crackling like newly lit flames in kindling wood.

By flattening ourselves against the wall, we managed to slide into the Avenue of the Revolution and down Neruda Street to our block. But it was no longer ours. It was burning. People zigzagged crazily to and fro, like ants from an overturned heap. For a second Aunt Natasha and I stood still. Everything suddenly seemed to me shifty and treacherous. I've never understood why anyone finds it difficult to believe chairs and tables are made of constantly moving atoms. Nothing is reliable in this moving world but love, and the loved die as easily as the unloved.

"Darling," I said stupidly, "are you alright?"

"Perfectly." But although she added, "Just as well we didn't have the radio mended in the circumstances," tears were running down Aunt Natasha's cheeks.

All at once the rushing to and fro stopped. Everyone

31

began streaming in the same direction, old people with bundles, women with babies, children with guns and toys, many of them crying or shouting, others staring blankly ahead, their shoulders hunched up. Tearing round a corner, the janitor's child butted into us. He carried a jug smelling of gasoline and shouted breathlessly: "Boris — looking for you — delicatessen."

Running through the smoke clouds, past the crumbling buildings and crazed people, we felt a horrid kind of relief: something we'd dreaded had happened, so there was that much less need for dread. Reliable as ever, Boris was standing on the delicatessen doorstep, peering into the smoke, his white hair on end, his face and riding boots the same reddish-brown. When I noticed the salami sticking out of his pocket, I nearly cried. It was so like him to have just what Aunt Natasha wanted at this minute.

"Natasha! Resi! My darlings! Where were you? Never mind now! Thank heaven you're here," and he tugged us out of the sea of smoke, round the corner, and down by the used canal, where he'd parked his horse box. In it were nine people and three horses. The driver started the engine as we climbed inside.

While we rumbled alongside the canal and, later, between snow-powdered stretches of furrowed brown land, everyone began discussing what was happening, not realizing what was, so that the talk was like a collective effort to do a huge jigsaw puzzle no one had ever seen completed. Aunt Natasha's black eye didn't look out of place here, as she sat up very straight, congratulating

Boris on having brought the horses along. She seemed to be feeling much better, and when Boris asked with anguish what would have happened if he hadn't found us, she replied with satisfaction, "Just as well I wasn't home this morning, in the circumstances, wasn't it?"

"Yes," Boris and I chorused, "yes, darling, it was." We would have said "yes, darling" to whatever she pronounced, so glad were we to have her here, black eye and all, all including the look of effrontery induced in her by a successfully overcome hangover. Watching Boris pat her shoulder in the fond way he keeps for her and horses, it struck me that one of his reasons for loving Aunt Natasha was the same as one of mine, namely he had never done anything to make him wish later that he'd been nicer to her. So, where she was concerned, he felt no remorse, only undiluted love.

When it grew dark, my head began to nod. Presently I fell asleep and, dreaming fitfully of the young man with a camera, was jolted through the darkness and across my first frontier, into another country.

CHAPTER TWO

When the rear flap of the horse box crashed down, gusts of cold damp air swirled in and a crowd of people pressed forward, some in uniform, some armed. After an instant's silence, they all began talking at once and continued, with increasing volume, until interrupted by Boris, who jumped out, his usually ruddy face pale in the moonlight, and caught their questions as a seal catches fish. We couldn't hear all the debate, but it wasn't long before Boris' expression changed to one of sly pleasure, as if he had pulled off an unexpected deal. Then he vaulted up, drew the flap after him, and on we went.

Presently we left the dirt track and began rumbling over stones. Edging round, I looked out front through a grating. We were in the middle of a city — or so I thought, seeing the shadowy outlines of twisted old houses with overhanging upper stories. Then we turned into a wider street of palatial buildings with carved grilles over their windows and escutcheons over their doors. A brilliant river of moonlight flowed down the middle of it, deepened here and there by golden squares reflected from lit-up shop windows. At home there are so few street lights that visitors and drunks often fall over the sidewalk after dark. In one of these shop windows, I could just see clusters of jewels like petrified flowers. I was wishing we could get hold of one —jewellery is so easy to hide, transport, and sell, though Aunt Natasha says one should place no reliance on pearls when it struck me that these were probably only display goods, like the pink cardboard pig with a wax apple in its mouth that has been in our butcher's window for as long as I can remember.

There were still plenty of people hurrying to and fro, some in fur coats, looking as purposeful as stage crowds at the opera, preparing for action during the overture. Then all at once, the lights went out. The transparent golden windows became darkly opaque, reflecting moonlit fragments of buildings and gliding movements like those of fish in an aquarium. Lights going out usually signify trouble, so I turned to see if Aunt Natasha looked as frightened as I felt. A ray of moonlight swept, like the hand of a demented clock, from one side of her face to the other, making her absent-minded smile look like a smile in what we were encouraged to call decadent modern abstract painting. Later, I discovered that she had been preoccupied just then by the problem of Sasha, Boris' recently lamed horse. When in great trouble, Aunt Natasha is apt to select a minor vexation and concentrate on this. Last time there was an abortive rising, a lion got sick in Boris' circus, and Aunt Natasha spoke so feelingly of noble animals pining, far from their natural habitat, that she almost convinced us the lion's predicament was worse than ours, and more interesting. By the time I'd discovered that this particular lion had been born and bred in a circus, the animal had recovered and there was no more street fighting in our district. Boris says this habit of Aunt Natasha's shouldn't be discouraged, as it is her form of mental therapy and doesn't prevent her from meeting disaster with courage.

The minute our horse box jolted to a standstill, more uniforms appeared, but mostly on women, unarmed. While I was thinking "officials" and seeing some of the sickening pictures that word conjures up, Boris said, "Ah, the Red Cross," sounding gratified and as if it were up to him to put everyone at ease. It has been said that if the devil showed up at his front door, Boris' first thought would be that the poor fellow must be tired after his long journey. Flickering torchlight and shifting shadows made every gesture mysterious as a conjurer's. Suddenly hands were clapped, and a peremptory voice asked what languages we possessed. When I said I knew some French, English, and German, the old woman from our delicatessen shop inquired so indignantly, "And how did you learn them?" that, instead of saying Aunt Natasha had taught me, I muttered "at school," which was plausible.

"Splendid," said the peremptory voice. "We shall have to enrol you as a helper."

My heart gave a thump. I didn't want to be enrolled in any capacity, anywhere. Just then Aunt Natasha winked at me and, looking round the big, cobbled square, I noticed a fountain decorated by statues of caracoling horses. Thinking of Boris' horses, I felt this to be a good omen, and remembered, too, that last time Olga told our fortunes she'd said we would shortly be going on a journey that would provide a solution for many problems.

Meanwhile, Boris was talking to a Red Cross man, gesticulating like a juggler, as if this were the only way to keep the foreign words flying. Before Aunt Natasha and I realized what was happening, he had hugged us, said, "Must see to the horses first — separate sleeping quarters for the men — will be round early tomorrow," climbed back into the horse box accompanied by the Red Cross man, and driven away. As he vanished, my knees began to tremble, and I remembered a story about a mother and daughter who went to Paris for an exhibition. After they had settled in the hotel where they'd booked a room, the girl went out on an errand for her mother. When she got back the room was empty – and the manager said there was no one of that name staying in the hotel. The mother had died of the plague, and the manager had hustled the body out by a back door so as not to frighten prospective customers. Perhaps Boris was being trapped into prison.

"Come on, my darling," said Aunt Natasha, in her whistling-in-the-dark voice. Keeping close to her, I followed the crowd into a large house with pale-yellow-light coming through its open front door. In the hall three Red Cross workers sat writing at tables covered with papers. As we shuffled past them, we were each given a square of cardboard with the word "refugee" written on it in capitals and, underneath, the date and a number.

When Anna from the delicatessen received her card, she held it up until it almost touched the tip of her big snub nose, and burst into noisy sobs. The woman who'd given her the piece of cardboard looked puzzled and exasperated as she asked what the matter was.

"The matter?" cried Anna indignantly. "It's this!" She stubbed her fat forefinger against the card just as she does when inspecting children's shopping lists in order to cry out at the exorbitance of their parents' demands. "This, this, this! To think I should live to hear myself called a refugee."

"But there's nothing dishonourable about being a refugee —"

"That only shows how little you know about refugees." Anna was shouting now. Like most shopkeepers never allotted enough goods to satisfy their customers, she always had raging self-defence ready to combat the slightest hint of adverse criticism. "Refugees! Dirty, nine times out of ten, prefer their own outlandish habits to ours, ungrateful like as not — and not above thieving. Refugees! My family's an honourable one, I'll have you know, my grandfather founded our store, built it up from nothing, and it's been in the family ever since — wars, risings, strikes, upsets, nothing's been able to dislodge us. And now . . . Suddenly her rage subsided, she looked down at the piece of cardboard, gave a hiccup-like sob and said, as if to herself, "I always thought refugees were other people." Then she sighed and, still speaking quietly, added "Never thought I'd see the day I'd be glad my man's not alive, but I am now, I wouldn't have had him see this for the world. He was so proud of the shop. Used to say that despite everything we offered the finest choice of sausages north of the Danube..."

"Who would have thought the old woman had so much blood in her?" whispered Aunt Natasha.

"What's that?"

"A misquotation from Shakespeare."

We had been reading Shakespeare's historical plays at school, and although he wrote over three centuries ago, in another country, and about royalty, his plots seemed full of actuality and perhaps for that reason were frightening. "How oft the sight of means to do ill deeds makes deeds ill done," for example, covers any police informer or persons officially paid for being wicked.

At the end of the passage was a door, its upper part made of coloured glass lozenges through which light came faintly, with sinister effect. In the huge room behind it, shadowy figures were lighting candles stuck into bottles. Now and again a uniform button caught the light and sparkled. Someone whispered that the electricity had fused. Later, I found this had been true; at the time I wondered why the speaker bothered to lie: so far as we were concerned it was too late for reassurance. Drafts kept the candle flames in motion, so that the mobile shadows made the room seem like a tent of billowing tapestries. The floor was scattered with straw, on which about thirty women and children, and several dogs, huddled asleep.

When we trooped in, a baby wailed and then stopped as if a hand had been clapped over its mouth, a dog growled softly, and from a tripped-over basket came indignant cluckings. This suddenly reminded me of a school debate on the subject of incubators. Ilona,

39

a star pupil, had spoken in favour of incubators, saying that hens who have never laid in so-called natural conditions don't know the difference, and that even if they did it would be criminally irresponsible to attribute more importance to the putative suffering of hens than to egg production. Then, to everyone's surprise, Ladislaus, a handsome, well-liked boy who sincerely believed almost everything we were told officially, declared himself in opposition and said it was wicked to keep hens shut up in boxes, with harsh light always in their eyes and electric shocks to provoke them to lay: an egg wasn't just something to eat, but the result of a hen's wandering in a barnyard with other creatures, stirring up dust just for the pleasure of it, enjoying the sun's warmth on its feathers, pecking officiously at nothings, communing with itself in small burping sounds; in other words, an egg was the result of a certain amount of hen's happiness. It was a good speech. But Ilona won. Afterwards, although he and I weren't in the same grade, Ladislaus suggested that we walk home together; I should have liked this, but it turned out that we lived in opposite directions. All this happened two years ago. Now, listening to the refugee hen's soft querulousness, I wondered what had happened to Ladislaus.

Having pushed two heaps of straw together, Aunt Natasha and I did what we call making spoons — that is, each lying on the right side, me in front, and Aunt Natasha's arms round my waist. We started this that winter when all the pipes froze and there was only black market fuel. By spreading both coats over us, we built a kind of tent. As we settled down, Aunt Natasha made a sign of the cross over me, which was unusual. The straw smelled pleasant, and as drowsiness spread through me I reflected that, whatever the truth of the matter, Mary and Joseph would surely have been astonished had anyone told them, when they were in that stable, that nearly two thousand years later people in distant countries would make the sign of the cross in remembrance of that baby and feel safer for having done so. I was half asleep when I suddenly became aware of Aunt Natasha's crying. Twisting round I whispered: "What is it? Oh, darling, don't . . ."

"Go to sleep, my pet, I wanted not to wake you."

"You didn't. I was thinking. Please tell me."

"You can't do anything, darling."

"I can sympathize."

Aunt Natasha's arms tightened around me. After a pause she said quietly, but with a despair that alarmed me, "Boris . . ."

Had Boris yearned for Aunt Natasha, I should have thought this natural, in keeping with his general attitude toward her; but she had always seemed to me to take him not exactly for granted — I knew that old and true affection united them — but with some of the detachment that marked her relations with everyone but me, for whom she felt the particular love one has for someone one has protected. When the Chinese want to wish anyone harm, they say, "May you live at an interesting period of history." Aunt Natasha had already lived through several interesting periods, and I think it was this that had developed detachment in her, the only alternative being bitterness, which wouldn't have suited her nature.

"He promised to come for us in the morning," I said. "He always keeps his promises."

"When he can . . . but suppose they won't let him?"

The fears that had kept after me ever since I was a child in nursery school, determined to follow Aunt Natasha's advice — never tell anyone a lie, but don't tell everyone the truth — pressed closer to me. Pushing back the tent, I leaned up on my elbow. In the pale flickering light Aunt Natasha's tear-ravaged face looked older than I'd ever seen it before. There were deep ash-coloured hollows under her eyes, deep folds in her thin neck.

"Suppose they won't let him," she repeated as if hypnotized. "Oh, I can't ... I cannot bear to live through that again."

In the past Aunt Natasha and I had often spent hours in conversations beginning "Tell me something about you I don't know." Thanks to lack of false modesty, she was very good at this: she loved hearing stories about anyone — if I hadn't wanted to supply her with fresh material, I should have paid far less attention to people at school — and she assumed that her own stories would be equally well received. So I knew a good deal about her, and although I realized her life contained much of which I was ignorant, I had assumed that this ignorance concerned only persons sealed up in her past — not Boris, who was part of our shared present.

This discovery of the strange in the familiar disturbed me more than anything else had since we crossed the frontier, and I worried about it until suddenly checked by the thought that I might have forgotten to turn the gas off before going to the Racnik. Presently I realized that, as our house was now rubble, a little more or less gas was of no importance. This stopped my worrying and almost immediately I fell asleep.

CHAPTER THREE

In my dream I was standing beside a lake, trying to lace my skating boots. The sound of the Skaters' Waltz increased my feverish longing to be on the ice, but suddenly my fingers refused to move. The music grew louder, became deafening, and I woke to hear the Skaters' Waltz blaring overhead. Turning, I found my eyes exactly level with a pair of large yellow boots.

These belonged to a big man in a purplish-grey suit, with thick black moustaches, the left one of which kept brushing against the violin he was strenuously playing. Dazed, I sat up and picked the straw out of my hair. Noticing me, the violinist grimaced a smile and bowed, without stopping playing. All round the room people were picking straw out of their hair, and standing among us were a score of performers, each equipped with a music stand and all playing fortissimo.

When the music stopped, I asked the man with the moustaches what was happening. After another grimace-smile he said that he and his colleagues from a small town just this side of the frontier had been temporarily evacuated, as a precautionary measure. They had in any case been due to give a concert here today, and as this was — here he coughed apologetically — this was in fact the municipal room used for rehearsals, they had been advised to carry on as usual.

"I suppose you don't smoke?" he asked, his head tilted as if playing the violin had given him a permanent crick in the neck.

"No, but my aunt, here, does."

"Would you like —"

"Yes, please."

He offered me a yellow cigarette with a cardboard filter, then said I could keep the whole pack. I accepted half, which amounted to six cigarettes, three for Aunt Natasha, three for Boris. Looking sad and guilty, the violinist asked where were we from? Before I could tell him, three metallic taps made him look away. The conductor raised his baton, and the *William Tell Overture* began thumping over us. This is music Aunt Natasha particularly dislikes, and she woke immediately, looking indignant even before her eyes were completely open.

"Deplorable! A really deplorable noise . . . Ah, there you are, darling." Smiling at me, she sat up, gently shaking straw from her hair. She didn't seem in the least surprised at being roused by an orchestra, only by that orchestra's choice of music.

"Why *William Tell*?" she asked. "Not that I've anything against him as a man, on the contrary, but this music would be an insult to an oppressor, let alone a liberator."

During a crescendo our Red Cross woman came in, looking distraught. She spoke to the conductor, who tapped his music stand, then stood still, glowering. The din had just ceased when a trombone player scattered a few last notes. Several people frowned at him, and he looked as embarrassed as if he'd belched on a platform during a speech by someone more important than himself. A few seconds later the musicians piled their stands and left.

Immediately afterwards a horde of women, children, babies, and some animals pressed into the room. They looked as we had last night, but more so. The first arrivals flung themselves on any unoccupied straw, and a foxy-looking dog rushed at the clucking basket and, after a preliminary sniff, began barking. The old woman who owned the basket screamed; so did two babies; and another dog, with a deep mournful bark, attacked the foxy one. Everyone began talking at once. One could hear truncated remarks. "What I always say is . . . it's disgraceful . . . enough trouble without . . . what I always say is ... no better than savages . . . some dogs are better citizens than . . . what I always say is . . ." Presently two Red Cross workers rushed in, separated the dogs, calmed the old woman, and, clapping their hands, proclaimed: "If you'll all sit down, rations will be served." As if by magic, everyone was seated and every face looked at the doorway, through which came the smell of food.

Slices of black bread and mugs of hot soup were distributed, and Aunt Natasha and I were lucky, each getting a big lump of potato in her share. We drank the soup and saved the bread. I showed Aunt Natasha the cigarettes. Delighted, she opened her coat, displaying a bottle of schnapps tucked inside. Boris had produced it in the horse box. "Let's go and find him." She seemed to have jumped over her nocturnal grief, perhaps because day is a less fearful time than night.

But the Red Cross people wouldn't let us out the front door. Not just yet, they said, apologetically at first, then irritated — all the more so because they clearly felt they ought not to be — by Aunt Natasha's insistence. "We know how you feel," they chorused, "we do indeed, and as soon as we've got everyone listed . . . but with so many pouring in . . . there's the medical aspect too ... so if you'll just wait . . ."

"Wait!" said Aunt Natasha, sounding imperious, disgusted, and so unlike her more usual self that I released I'd been mistaken in thinking she'd surmounted last night's grief. Waiting has always been as much a part of our life as rationing, queuing, or filling in forms, and Aunt Natasha is generally calmer about this than I am.

Grumbling softly, Aunt Natasha went back to the door of our dormitory. Then as soon as she was sure no one was watching us, she started down a passage leading to the back of the house. It was a wide but twisty passage, scattered with disparate objects: a billiard table with a hole in its green baize, a broken-nosed plaster cherub, a coat stand with deer's antlers supporting a couple of *Pickelhaube* helmets, a stuffed peacock with a dusty Tyrolese hat over its head and neck, a bronze figure of a man playing a violin, and several pairs of skis. Presently we found a cupboard underneath a staircase. It contained brooms, brushes, cloths, and pails, and also room for us. We upturned two pails and sat down behind the bamboo curtain that served as a door. With one of the cloths I cleaned our boots, while Aunt Na-

47

tasha put the bread and schnapps on a third upended pail. Then she lit a cigarette. We felt triumphant at having achieved privacy.

"We shall hear Boris," said Aunt Natasha confidently. "When he doesn't find us in that dormitorium, he'll examine the rest of the house." She raised the bottle and poured some schnapps down her throat.

"Darling, why did you say 'again' last night about Boris not being with us? Were you thinking of that time when he was on tour with the circus?" I asked.

"Oh no, long before that. You weren't born then, my darling."

"Oh . . ." Aunt Natasha had not talked of the far-off past for a long time and, as she sounded melancholy, I said uncertainly, "Well, at least that's over and done with now."

Aunt Natasha shook her head. "Nothing's ever over." She held the bottle of schnapps to the light and squinted at it. "Because everything has prolongations in time. Repercussions. There's no escaping continuity. If I'd married Boris when I ought to have, for example, we wouldn't be here now."

"Where would we be?"

"Russia, Italy, America, maybe dead — but not here. Incidentally, darling, did you keep that bit of cardboard they gave you last night?"

I nodded.

"No idea what I did with mine. Do you think it matters?"

"Probably not," I said, although in my experience anything to do with papers always matters more than the papers' owners do. I fully expect to be ordered to fill in a form when I come to die. Not wishing to dwell on this, I asked, "When should you have married Boris? And why didn't you?"

"Because when I was your age, I was very foolish. By which I do not mean I was a joyous madcap, a practical joker. No, I was silly in an earnest way. I had no sense of proportion. Injustice repelled me, and the least exhibition of unkindness made me deeply melancholy. Yet whenever a handsome young man complimented me, life ceased to be a vale of tears, and I was beside myself with joy. My French governess used to say that I was *pas sérieuse*, and she was justified that winter in Petersburg when my brother Yakov unexpectedly came on leave."

"You never told me you'd had a brother," I said, taken aback. Perhaps because I had so few relatives, a brother still seemed to me more important than a lover; and even today I tend to overestimate love's fraternal elements.

"There was no reason."

Wondering why, if there had been none before, there was reason now, I said, "Except that a brother of yours must be very unlike Uncle Matthias, and I'd be glad to have more than one relative not like Uncle Matthias."

"That Yakov certainly was. But he's been dead a long while, and until now Uncle Matthias was a safer connection for you." Here she peered through the bamboo curtain to make sure no one could overhear us. It did not take much alcohol to make Aunt Natasha scent conspiracies all around us. But on more than one occasion she had been proved right, as when she declared that the janitor's cousin was a police informer and not long afterwards he was found stabbed to death in an alley behind the wartime Thief Market. In some respects Aunt Natasha was more clairvoyant than Olga. "Please go on about your brother," I said anxiously.

"Yakov was one of the most charming human beings I've ever known—good-looking, goodhearted, no fool. A typical young officer at a time when war was still rather more the concern of soldiers than of scientists."

Depression seized me. This was the kind of antiscientific remark often made by older people, but never until now by Aunt Natasha. I didn't mind her being antiscientific, nor anti-anything else she wanted to be, but her showing signs of age upset me. As if sensing this, she quickly added, "Of course, war was just as wicked then as now; being killed by a bomb, whatever its formula, is neither physically nor morally worse than having a bayonet thrust in one's stomach."

"Or a tank."

"Or a tank. But there used to be more scope for individual exploits. Well, it was near the feast of Saint Nicholas when Yakov arrived. The cold took one's breath away; hats froze on people's heads; and once the Christmas market on the Neva started — a mile of booths either side; oh, how pretty it looked — then great expanses of the river were reserved for skating. Yakov was a wonderful skater — how we two skated!"

Something in her tone made me shiver. I tried to look

through Aunt Natasha as she was now — tired, creased, witchlike on a pail, a broom in one hand, a bottle of schnapps in the other— to that young girl skimming between the festive booths on the Neva. Trying to exorcise distress by concentrating on something practical., I asked, "Did you buy things at the market booths?"

Aunt Natasha shook her head. "I didn't need things in those days."

"I see." But it was easier to imagine a mile of glittering shops on a frozen river than a state in which one didn't need things.

"What Yakov and I liked was to get away from the crowds, past the washerwomen kneeling beside holes in the ice —"

"Didn't the washerwomen freeze?"

"No. They used to say they were accustomed to it. But they had a poor reputation as washers. Rich people sent their laundry to London."

They sent their laundry to London? School and reading had given me a rough idea of the errors of the old regime, but no account of justly revenged oppression had made the difference between then and now as vivid to me as did the notion of dirty clothes crossing a continent.

"Yakov and I used to make friends with the washerwomen because we were fascinated by their holes in the ice. It was rumored that murderers used them for dumping bodies, and murder still seemed unusual to girls raised as I had been. Well, soon after Benediction —"

"What was that?"

"Benediction of the Waters, in front of the Winter Palace, on January sixth, in memory of the baptism of Christ. Soon after that Yakov invited home a younger friend, a brother officer: Boris."

"Was that the first time you met him?"

"No, oh no, that was just the trouble."

"How do you mean?"

"I was so ready to admire Yakov's friends that had I met Boris for the first time then I should undoubtedly have fallen in love with him. But unfortunately he was the son of old friends of my parents, and I'd known him as a shy adolescent in civilian clothes. My pacifism didn't prevent my admiring soldiers."

"You didn't like Boris?" Feeling betrayed, I squeezed Aunt Natasha's hand to show her I felt nothing of the sort.

"Yes indeed, we were devoted to each other, rather as you and I are."

"What could be better?"

"Nothing, my pet. As you realize, being young, and as I realize, being old; but in between there are stages at which devotion does not suffice. Boris was like a brother, and I didn't need another brother just then. I needed to tremble, to yearn, to feel myself part of a drama, you understand."

With my mind I understood, but with nothing else. I had never wanted to be part of a drama. On the contrary. Drama alarms me, except in art, safely framed, between covers.

"Go on," I said.

"Gradually I realized from hints and looks – a suspicious amount of attentiveness to me – that my parents intended me to marry Boris. I discovered later that Boris' parents had for years wanted him to marry me, but my parents had thought his fortune inadequate. Now his older brothers had been killed in a railway accident, so Boris was well off, and both our parents were in agreement."

"I suppose Boris loved you then just as he does now?" As usual I longed for evidence of stability.

"Not as he does now." Her laugh was mischievous, indulgent. Aunt Natasha and I laughed a great deal together, and I liked all her ways of laughing—even her drunken one had a kind of joyous gusto — but it hadn't struck me before, as it did now, that no woman could laugh as she laughed without having once been sure of arousing admiration, bestowing pleasure.

"Whenever I spoke to other young men," she continued, her words soaked in laughter, "or danced with them, Boris became pale and furious and despairing—"

"Then why did you?"

"Because I liked him to look pale and furious and despairing. What I cared about then was not him, but his effect on me, mine on him. I was still at the stage of wanting to try life as a boy tries the edge of a new pocket-knife."

Melancholy swept over me like cold air. I had never wanted anyone to look pale and furious and despairing on my account, and couldn't imagine doing so. Usually,

I felt quite proud of the common sense developed in me by the fact that a household must contain one person who can mend fuses; but now this common sense seemed to me something poor and makeshift, shockingly inferior to the emotions common to Aunt Natasha and the older ballets.

"So you treated him badly?" I asked. Then I heard the admiration in my voice and blushed, not from shame or embarrassment but from annoyance, as one does after unintentionally saying the opposite of what one meant.

Aunt Natasha nodded, drank some schnapps, and said,

"I felt so sure," she added, "that no matter how badly I behaved he would understand that it meant nothing. But of course he didn't."

"Why of course?" Had Boris too been very unlike his present self?

"Because he had his own feelings to grapple with. When one's very young and in love, one's so dazzled by one's own feelings that one has in fact very little eyesight to spare for the other person. It's the time of egotistical love."

So far, I hadn't thought much about love, other than domestic love. Schoolwork and my share of the housekeeping kept me busy, and Aunt Natasha and I were so contented together that I had very little unemployed imagination. I expected to marry, just as I expected to grow a centimetre or two more; but, perhaps because I also expected marriage to involve housing and other problems not mentioned in connection with love by

Pushkin or Shakespeare, I had never felt drawn to soft ruminations on the subject. My sexual instincts were still unaroused, and to me, love meant Aunt Natasha.

"What happened then?"

"Something dreadful."

Immediately thinking of fatal accidents, I felt a great weariness. People sometimes speak of the monotony of life, but this seems to me negligible compared with the monotony of death. In the Middle Ages artists often painted allegorical pictures representing the Dance of Death; but if I were a painter now I would paint a nonallegorical picture with naked men, women, and children, their ribs showing clearly under their grimy skin, all packed close as pickled herrings in a gas chamber, waiting for death from unnatural causes. As always when I thought of concentration camps, I trembled internally, partly from anger and partly from fear, each emotion increasing the other.

"It started harmlessly enough," admitted Aunt Natasha. "Always beware, my darling, of things that start harmlessly. It started by our going to the theatre to see a visiting French company play Racine's *Bérénice*."

"The Emperor Titus gives up Queen Bérénice, whom he loves, because he puts his duty to his country first?"

"That's right." Aunt Natasha's tone suggested that she saw nothing right about it. "The actor who played Titus was the handsomest man I'd ever seen, and he had something I was not then equipped to recognize as animal magnetism. I was, however, equipped to feel it. Unfortunately, he was of quite a good upper-class

55

family in spite of being an actor — that was the way my family talked, and so did everyone we knew —so we met him socially and, naturally, I fell madly in love with him. I use the word madly advisedly," said Aunt Natasha, pausing, a long nicotine-stained forefinger upraised, "because the unreality of the situation kept my feelings flying the way a balloon is kept up by air. Beware of passions for actors unless you're an actress. When Bérénice said:

Dans un mois, dans un an, comment souffrirons nous,
Seigneur, que tant de mers me séparent de vous...

I sobbed aloud, to the gratification of my French governess. Not even my mother realized what this signified; having made up her mind I was to marry Boris, she thought I was no more in need of surveillance than a pie safely out of the oven. So when we met socially I was able to talk to Titus without arousing unfavorable comment at home."

"His name wasn't really Titus?"

"No, but, do you know, I can't remember exactly what it was. Let me see . . ."

This gave me a shock. Knowing the goodness of Aunt Natasha's heart, I could not but think her memory must be failing. Then she relieved me by adding: "Yes, I can. It's just come back to me; his Christian name was Louis. I remember it well, because I used to call him Alexis. And I ran away with him."

"Where to?"

"Paris. That, at least, was our intention. But don't get the idea poor Alexis was a scheming seducer. Someone once said that in such cases the victim is nearly always the culprit, and I certainly was. Alexis really meant to marry me in Paris. Like many successful actors, he was deeply bourgeois and behaved in a most respectful manner once my maid and I were settled in the sleeping car for Königsberg."

"Your maid?"

"That's the kind of thing I meant when I said I was very foolish at your age. I could imagine running away from home, crossing Europe with a stranger, breaking Boris' heart, upsetting my family, but it hadn't occurred to me that I might manage to dress myself without a maid."

As I nodded, thinking of the laundry sent to London, Aunt Natasha glanced at her clothes and at mine — our coarse straw-bedizened sweaters, rumpled skirts, thread stockings, heavy boots — and suddenly burst out laughing. Without knowing why, I joined in. We laughed and laughed, tears pouring down our cheeks. Whenever one of us managed to stop for a few minutes, the other was overcome by a wild uncontrollable laughter that attacks a school class when a teacher says, "There's nothing whatever to laugh at."

"I think we're growing hysterical," said Aunt Natasha with interest.

"Go on. So there you were in the Königsberg sleeper —"

"So delighted with my compartment that I almost forgot Alexis. It had such a neat plump sofa that turned into a bed with a spring mattress. I'd never had one to myself before, only shared with a cousin who kicked in her sleep. We had about thirty hours' worth of cornfields and fir woods, stopping occasionally at little stations where we were given glasses of tea and lemon. At night I looked out of the window for bears and wolves, which seemed to me essential to an elopement, but all I saw was my own misty reflection in the glass. We got to Wierzbolow, at the frontier, without trouble, and I jumped out in a mood of the greatest exhilaration. Everything seemed to me delightful, delicious; not only Alexis and the life we would lead in Paris, but the faint winter sunlight making the snow sparkle, the porters with their long white aprons, scarlet shirts, and huge jack boots, until the stationmaster appeared, flanked by local officials, and respectfully announced he had orders I was to return to Petersburg, and Alexis to leave Russia at once."

"Oh darling!"

"Yes. No need to invent bears and wolves on the return journey. Next time I saw Alexis — oh, years later that was — I remembered his having told me in the train that when making one's face up for an old part one must draw a line from the inner corner of the eyebrow to the outer corner of the eye, to create the illusion of sagging flesh." For a second Aunt Natasha laid her fingers on the place where her own flesh now sagged, giving her still beautiful shining eyes the look of young prisoners in an old building. "By that time poor Alexis didn't need grease paint to create an illusion of age."

"What happened when you got home?"

"Well, there was no suggestion, as I had hoped there might be, that a treasure had almost been lost. Once the family doctor had declared I was as good as new where my matrimonial prospects were concerned, my father treated me to embarrassed silence, my mother to irony and contempt. Even Yakov was angry, on Boris' account."

"Were you very unhappy?"

"Very? No. Despite all the unpleasantness, I couldn't take my disgrace altogether seriously. I was very immature for my age, so none of my actions seemed to me final, and I thought it odd of other people to behave as if they were."

"What about Boris?"

"He was away on duty, and I wasn't allowed to write or receive letters until some months later, when I was told that in order that I should not bring further disgrace on my family whom God knows had done nothing to deserve it, I was being given an undeserved opportunity to marry a friend of my father's. I was in no mood to appreciate a middle-aged man with an old name, a passion for hunting, and what people like us used to call 'no money.'" Here she laughed and shook her head. "But I saw no alternative and did like the idea of being a married woman. Besides, I thought Boris would rue the day when he came back and found me married."

"You still wanted to make him despair?"

"Yes, but now I intended to make it up to him. I had grown up a little. I didn't expect my future husband to occupy much of my time, and for once I was right.

When he wasn't hunting, he was shooting or fishing, which meant he came home so sleepy that he was barely capable of climbing into his own bed. Poor fellow, I grew very fond of him. He gave me a pet raccoon."

"But I thought he was a general."

"Oh no. It was my second husband who was a general."

"Your second husband? But what about Boris?"

"What about him indeed," boomed Boris' voice, as he flung aside fistfuls of bamboo curtain. "And what are you two doing here? I was quite distracted when I couldn't find you. I've been prowling all over the house, and a very odd place it is, there's a room upstairs full of stuffed owls and Nuremberg musical boxes. What were you doing, darlings?"

"Talking of the past," said Aunt Natasha.

Boris groaned. "Your sense of timing has always been arbitrary, but . . ."

"Have some schnapps, my dear, and this," she handed him bread, "is for you."

"And I'd brought this for you." He produced a slice of pumpernickel. "Excellent stabling they've given us. Come on, let's get out of here."

"No good trying the front door just now," I warned him.

"I know. I've been investigating the position. There's a lavatory down the passage with a large low window overlooking a quiet back street. No snoopers."

"You're so thorough," said Aunt Natasha.

A few minutes later we were all three walking cautiously down Boris' snooperless street.

CHAPTER FOUR

It had rained earlier, but now the sun was shining, and green roof tiles, gilded shop signs, immaculate plate glass threw off sparks of refracted light, so that the air seemed to be alive with golden confetti. Although I couldn't remember a time when we three had had less reason for gaiety I was suddenly and unthinkingly happy as once, years ago, when Boris took us on tour with him, and we slept in a caravan and woke to the sound of tigers stretching their throats in huge slow yawns.

Neither Boris nor Aunt Natasha spoke at first, but tilted their faces to the cool bright sunshine with tentative enjoyment, like convalescents. Anxious to discover what was happening, yet dreading doing so, we walked circumspectly, trying to prolong this moment, to limit our attention to our linked arms and the sunshine on our faces.

Halfway down the next street, which was full of traffic — I'd never before seen so many motor vehicles in one place — we were attracted by a prodigious delicatessen store. The vast window's centrepiece was a glass-fronted silver machine in which a chicken roasted on a revolving spit. Either side stood massive hams, their outsides neatly bread-crumbed, their insides the colour of dark-pink roses. Spread around these in tiers were shallow white china dishes containing black and green olives, soft-fleshed tan mushrooms, smooth-skinned coppery sausages, the harlequin colours of vegetable salad, artichokes with grey-green mauve-topped leaves firm as if sculpted, beetroots with their darkly crimson juice turned cherry colour where it dissolved into a moat of sour cream, pies with richly glazed and crusted tops.

"What will it be?" asked Boris, with a look of modest triumph.

"We haven't got any of this money," I said regretfully.

Boris put his hand in his pocket and produced a jingling sound.

"There's something to be said for the habits acquired by a lifetime of looting," said Aunt Natasha.

"You overestimate me, my dear. In fact, I was paid the day before yesterday and had the money on me, and a jockey down at the stables changed it. What shall we have?"

"Pie's best for eating with fingers."

We bought three slices of pork pie, and two bottles of beer, to be kept for later. We ate the pie as we walked, chewing each mouthful as long as possible and not dropping a crumb. As she finished hers, Aunt Natasha gave a sigh of pleasure and said: "'If you give them money they only spend it on drink.' The kind of remark that does more than a peck of injustice to cause a revolution."

"We'd certainly better spend this money," said Boris, "otherwise it may be taken off us or devalued. Refugees are pouring in."

"And being sent where?" In spite of sunshine and pie, I was still full of dread.

"Nowhere. We're not allowed to move for the moment. Otherwise," Boris sounded apologetic, "this country would be overrun — we're in the position of rabbits."

"What ought we to do?"

"Stay put." Boris looked from one to the other of us, almost accusingly. "Some who came across yesterday are already talking of going back."

"What did they leave behind?"

"Their hearts. So they think now." Boris spoke angrily, for him. "But I don't want either of you listening to oratory. Though you ought to be used to it by now. In so far as in us lies, we three are going to stay together — and stay put. From now on they can count us out. You and I are too old, Natasha."

"We've left our hearts across frontiers before," she agreed.

"And Resi's too young."

"People younger than I am fight." I thought of that fifteen-year-old partisan whom they hanged in the forest.

"Do you want to fight, Resi?"

For a second I hesitated. One is often told that it's difficult to speak the truth, but it seems to me that the difficulty lies in accepting the truth oneself before speaking. Dishonesty being contagious, I should not have admitted at school that I dreaded fighting, hated and feared violence. But here, beside Aunt Natasha and Boris, I could accept my cowardice and admit that all I wanted right now was for us three to be left together, to be left alone.

"Just stick to that," said Boris, anxiety in his voice and look. I took his arm. Presently he relaxed and said, "I suggest we find a café where we can read the papers. That will be our best way of finding out what's happening. I seem to remember a big place in the center of town where no one pays any attention to anyone else."

"Have you been here before?" I asked, surprised.

"A long time ago. When I was another person, and it was another country. But I dare say the café is still there. Cafés are likely to outlast governments."

"One of the few facts that suggest man is not completely insane," said Aunt Natasha.

She and Boris smiled at each other, and suddenly I saw a young girl skating with a young officer in a Russian city of glittering bulbous roofs. Their narrowly booted feet slid forward, leaving silver tracks on the ice's powdery surface. They were as vivid to me as if my own memory had supplied the picture, and when I looked from them to Boris and Aunt Natasha in their present state, the latter were aureoled for me by the fact of owning pasts in which there had been enough love to allow for emotional extravagance. Knowing myself incapable of it, I particularly admired extravagance, and this admiration gave my love for them a new dimension. They had always satisfied me; now they disturbed my imagination. I had always loved them as they were; now I was falling in love with what they had been.

Boris' café was still where he had left it and not, he said, much altered: a comfortable place with steamy plate-glass windows, damson-coloured chairs plushily upholstered, shining spittoons, and potted plants. A tiny, yellow-eyed boy in a green baize apron was polishing leathery leaves with drops of liquid which he carefully shook onto a red cloth. Big gilt-framed mirrors, which gave the room visual extensions, had plump nymphs enamelled over their surfaces, and no one seemed to be spying on anyone else. Which didn't prevent our choosing the table furthest from everyone, just to be on the safe side. On it was a bowl half full of lumps of sugar, which we quickly divided and pocketed.

Boris and Aunt Natasha ordered beer, and I had chocolate, which came in a thin china cup. This tasted rather different from thick china, and very different from plastic. A little way behind where we sat hung a score of newspapers, each fastened into a chunky wooden stick with a metal hook at its top. Having fetched several of these, Boris gave us each one. Smiling at a Swiss paper, Aunt Natasha said, "Do you remember that day in Geneva? Resi must see Geneva sometime."

She had never before spoken as if there were any likelihood of my traveling. Now here we were abroad, and, all at once, it was home that seemed foreign, the unfamiliar home evoked in big letters on the front pages of the unfamiliar newspapers drooping like flags at half-mast from their wooden spines. Reading the dogmatic headlines patrolled by exclamation marks, I could think only of details unmentioned here: a policeman smiling dreadfully on a doorstep where he was not welcome; a ragged toothless old woman mending a useless chair beside a wrecked tank; the smell of human sweat and of horses', the former more acid, the latter more pungent; the crackling sound of burning and the sensation of smarting eyelids. From such fragments of confusion these papers had created a "long-expected uprising" about which everything was clear at a first reading — but less so at a second one. Long expected by whom? By "all thinking people" said one paper, in an article illustrated by a photograph of crowds shaking their fists. "That's the spirit" was the caption under this. "The eyes of the world" were upon us, stated another paper. Looking around I saw that the eyes nearest us were turned towards a chessboard, and that the barman was meditatively polishing tumblers, occasionally holding one up to the light and smiling at its soap-bubble surface.

Looking round the room I felt fiercely glad of the players' absorption in their chessmen, of the look of complicity the barman gave his glasses, of the yellow-eyed boy's careful polishing of the leaves — of all these evidences of private preoccupations. Boris remarked that we'd better check on happenings at our billets. At this point we wondered what we ought to do about tipping. At home tipping is forbidden but, generally speaking, only party members in good standing can afford to stick to this rule – though waiters have to be careful whom they take tips from.

It was just after passing the royal stables, which Boris pointed out to me with pride — nothing concerning animals is alien to him — that we collided with Ladislaus, carrying a rucksack and looking wretched. Seeing us he turned first red, then white, and began shouting greetings and slapping our backs, "What's happening?" we asked him, while he was asking us.

Shaking his head and running his hands over his elbows, Ladislaus said that on "that morning" — already these words held particular significance for us; until the next disaster we would date events in our lives as before or after "that morning" — on that morning, then, Ladislaus had stayed home late to watch his cactus, one that flowers only every four years and was due to do so around then. Ladislaus had for this plant the feelings of both a lover and a policeman, and when at last he had to go out, to pick up tickets for the Saturday football game, he'd run all the way. Yes, the streets had been a bit emptier than usual. But he hadn't paid too much attention to this at the time, what with the cactus and the football game. Ladislaus paused, shook his head gloomily, said, "It's probably flowering now," tugged at his right ear, and added incredulously, "Saturday's today, isn't it?" Then he went back to yesterday, when he had found the ticket office shut, which it had no business to be at that hour, and as he ran home he noticed a shop with a broken window, so immediately crossed the street, because thanks to the current obsession with juvenile delinquency anyone under twenty needs to watch other people's steps. On the way he had run into our chemistry master, who had collected half a dozen boys and urged Ladislaus to join them. At the time he hadn't been quite clear what it was all about. But now here he was. "I always act without thinking," he concluded sadly.

"Not this time, you didn't," said Boris.

Our lavatory window was still open, and Aunt Natasha and I got back to the main room without our absence rousing more than a few suspicious glances from persons who feared we might have been securing advantages. Once one is a refugee, one starts developing an exaggerated form of queue mentality. I could already feel it in myself. I would have gone to any lengths to secure an advantage, however unfairly, for Aunt Natasha.

The owner of the most belligerent dog, and the woman with the hen, had come to an agreement. The dog was kept tethered when the hen took the air, which it was doing now, wandering in small circles, ruffling its dusty orange-brown feathers, stretching its metallic-looking legs in a meditative way, and every now and again producing a sound like a cuckoo clock about to strike. The old woman tore a cabbage leaf into little bits and the hen ate these avidly yet with disgust, looking jerkily up and around in a sardonic manner. It squawked loudly when reinterned in the basket, and the dogs, lying under the piano with their tongues hanging out, appeared to exchange glances.

Just then a Red Cross woman came and asked if we were all vaccinated. By chance, Aunt Natasha and I had been done recently and, before going to the Racnik, I'd put the certificates in my purse on the you-never-can-tell principle. Some people immediately bared their arms and held them out, others cried that it was not their fault, others simply cried. Although vaccination

69

is compulsory at home, some of the peasants still try to evade it on the grounds that it is the mark of the beast. The dogs barked, and an old woman exclaimed in a plummy but resonant voice that God would punish them and us, nodding to herself as if she found this very satisfactory.

Rumors began spreading like circles round the spot where a stone has dropped into a pond. The room grew stuffy with fear. People hurled questions at their neighbours but went on talking through the answers. Someone said they were burning everything, someone else that, on the contrary, they had been taught a lesson. An emotional voice expressed a wish to go home and spoke of rats and sinking ships, whereupon an even more emotional voice flared up and said, "Speak for yourself," and the words "Huns, Mongolians, Tartars, barbarians" flew through the air like shapes of things to come. Just then a siren went off, making us jump and clutch each other. Feeling in her pocket, Aunt Natasha found a piece of bread and pressed it into my hands.

"Have you noticed that one's appetite grows as food gets scarcer? I don't know why people are constantly extolling nature's way."

"But we've had a lot to eat here."

"That won't last."

"Why not?" I asked stupidly, trying not to listen for the bombs I expected to follow the siren.

"Because people soon get tired of refugees. The pattern seldom varies. First welcoming looks, eager handclasps, food and drink, all sincerely offered. They not only mean but want to wash our feet. But if crises last too long, if there are too many of us for existing charitable organizations — and there always are — then refugees are suddenly discovered to be ungrateful and given to intrigues. And of course we often are. We start by bringing out the best in some people, and end by bringing out the worst in everyone. I didn't tell you this before, because back home it would have caused you nothing but nagging regret, but do remember now that whenever they close frontiers and stop individual travel, voluntary travel, which produces pleasure and commerce, then the next thing is mass involuntary travel — refugees — which produces only trouble. Look at us."

The siren was mute now, and no bomb had fallen within earshot. Suddenly a door was slammed, footsteps rattled down the passage, hands were clapped, and a harassed voice said, "All together, please! Together. Don't let's have any stragglers. We want everyone out of here in half an hour."

The voice continued explaining, but I stopped listening. Aunt Natasha was right. They were tired of us already, and although they were neither not responsible for our plight, nor under an obligation to assist us, I felt angry, which I hadn't yesterday: angry and frightened, and therefore eager to be unfair. The first stage of our outward journey was accomplished, and I was no longer an innocent traveller.

PART TWO

'The miserable have no other medicine
But only hope'
WILLIAM SHAKESPEARE, *Measure for Measure*

CHAPTER FIVE

Huddled outside was a crowd of people in clothes that, though of different shades, now looked predominantly dun-grey. White-knuckled hands clutched nervously at suitcases, bundles, rucksacks, and baskets, and distress made every face angular. An official voice, as rational as its owner's uniform, explained that we were only being transferred to the other side of town because these premises were actually needed for incoming refugees; things must be organized in stages, the screening process, buses will be provided, now will everyone just cooperate? But the voice's moderation was powerless against the tornado of rumours.

Next to me an old woman, crying almost silently, whispered, "They're going to send us back." Immediately, a long-chinned neighbour contradicted her. "To a camp, more likely," she said, then added briskly, as if deriving gratification from her own bitterness, "I knew we shouldn't escape. All my family've died in camps. We're intended for the crematorium, all right." At the word "crematorium" the weeping woman gave the beginning of a thin scream, but quickly popped her rheumatism-twisted hand over her mouth. "Nothing personal intended," grumbled the woman whose family had died in camps. "What kind of talk is that?" asked a dog owner. "Why exaggerate? So ungrateful. Enough to provoke destiny." An argument started. But instead of spreading, as it usually does in crowds — those who know nothing about the matter under discussion being the most vociferous — this was restricted to half a dozen voices. The rest of us merely pressed closer together, trying to oppose destiny.

There were lampposts all along the street, and I told myself that if I could count them before the return of the uniformed woman, who had gone indoors to look for a missing number, then everything would be all right. I knew nothing could make everything all right, but this did not prevent my being relieved when I won my bet with myself. At last, two big blue autocars drove round the corner, stopping in front of us. Instinctively we all drew back, as if these vehicles were dangerous animals crowned with luggage racks. Along the autocars' smooth blue sides were metal letters, the words "Tours" and "Venice" catching the light. As we climbed into the second one, I asked Aunt Natasha if she had ever been to Venice, and she nodded. "One's eyes are never hungry there; churches like great pearls, trees springing out of marble, the sound of water lapping against stone and, in the autumn, the taste of mushrooms and walnuts and cheese — the Venetians used to call tourists 'the Autumn People.'"

I had longed to travel before, but only spasmodically, as one longs for the unobtainable. Now, beginning to be aware of the colours Aunt Natasha had kept to herself in order not to disturb the equilibrium of our drabness, I felt as if I'd helped condemn a concert pianist to play nothing but five-finger exercises.

Squeezing her hand, I whispered, "Maybe we'll go

there together one day?"

"We're moving in the right direction. But," looking worried, "Venice is not a good place for horses. Even the fire engines are motorboats."

We were driving through what seemed to be back streets. There was scarcely more traffic than at home and, here and there, fingers of grass showed between cobbles, wisps of straw blew out from wooden doorways, and a group of children stopped singing "Ringel, Ringel, Rosenkrantz" to stare as we passed. Then back to macadamized surfaces, traffic stagnant between cliflike warehouses. Here the road was blocked by trucks, their drivers leaning out and exchanging insults and spittle. Next came more shops, well-covered women carrying baskets, and the road widening into a huge statued platz with a great church spiring up on the other side, its roof grass-green.

Sunlight had made way for greyness, and it was evening when at last we stopped in a narrow street of brick houses, old-fashioned rather than old, with nibbled stucco around doors and windows. We climbed out into a snow-carrying wind and were marshalled through an outer door of wood, an inner one of glass, to into a hall decorated with photographs of men in frock coats and commanding attitudes. There were also several notice boards. Even without these, one would have known this was a school from the smell of chlorine, chalk, and stale clothes. As our footsteps echoed down the linoleumed passage I half expected to hear a familiar voice cry "In step! Watch your step!"

The room where we were to sleep was very large, and contained army blankets as well as straw. Having arranged ours, Aunt Natasha and I sat down and did what Elsa's father called "casing the joint." Wooden bars striped the opposite wall, and in front of them stood a vaulting horse, a springboard, and a basket of Indian clubs. Ropes hanging from the ceiling were looped to the walls. I hoped we shouldn't be awakened by gyrating athletes.; better the William Tell. By this time my dread of change had swelled to include even change for the better.

Suddenly my heart missed a beat. "Did we leave the schnapps in our broom cupboard?"

Aunt Natasha patted her coat. Reassured, my thoughts returned to her past. As we waited for cabbage soup, the smell of which was drifting into the room, I asked, "Darling, didn't you see Boris again between your marriages?"

"But of course. I saw him again soon after my first marriage — and realized I had made a terrible mistake. But by then I had grown up enough to know my own foolishness was to blame, not my kind old husband, - who shouldn't therefore be made to pay for the damage. In fact, I'd I had grown very fond of Anton. He allowed me to carry out all my plans for our peasants — which was more than they themselves did—and even took me traveling, which meant many sacrifices from a sportsman's point of view, although of course our itineraries included a certain amount of animal slaughter. In those days it was the world that excited me, the sight of it, the state of it, the feel of it…for several years the mere fact of existence kept me delirious with sensation."

"But Boris?"

"Still in the army. We had parted sorrowfully yet pleased with ourselves. When one's young, one can get a great deal of satisfaction out of an attitude, providing one's not hungry. Later on it seemed impossible that I hadn't missed Boris, but at the time I wasn't dissatisfied with what I had. Inside the close quarters of marriage one is bound to love unless one hates — and I didn't hate Anton. I came to have the tenderest feelings for him, and I shall never forget his gentleness when my mother died."

"You mean my grandmother?"

"No, my father married again. Your grandmother was his second wife, Maria."

"Did you know her?"

"Very well. As a girl I greatly admired her. She was the daughter of Czech friends of ours — their country was still part of the Austro-Hungarian empire in those days, so you see one's always in trouble of some kind — and she held views, which my mother considered unsuitable in a young girl. Maria was only a few years older than myself. She was tall and sallow, with beautiful yellow-flecked dark eyes, rather like yours. And there was something about her that suggested a captive — a fierce captive for whose imprisonment one was in some mysterious way responsible. At first I thought, or rather hoped, she had won disapproval by falling unsuitably in love. Then one day she horrified me by declaring love a waste of time, though she did soften this by adding 'as society is organised now.' She was a member of the intelligentsia, and made a point of speaking Russian."

"Why not?"

"People of our kind usually spoke French. But Maria thought that wrong, like the way society was organized."

"Did you agree?"

"Society, yes. Not so specifically, but…I had a feeling that something…somehow – it was very vague – was coming to a climax…needed watching…you know how it is when milk's boiling, no matter how low the gas is, if you take your eye off it for a second the milk promptly boils over."

"Did your father — my grandfather — feel that too?"

"Until my mother's death, father sincerely believed everything a person of his class was expected to believe. Then loneliness made what amounted to a chemical change in him. He became a reading addict, discovering ideas as boys discover stamps; and Maria's fierce young believingness was one of these stamps. Before he knew where he was, clandestine leaflets were as thick inside the house as autumn leaves outside and, shuffling eagerly among them, he became reacclimatised to love."

"What was my father like as a child?"

"I didn't see him until much later, after we'd left Russia."

"You mean he was against the revolution?" I asked, excited, shocked, frightened.

"Your father was six years old at the time and there

are no counter-revolutionaries of six."

"But his parents - "

"I didn't hear the details until later. At the beginning of the 1914 War my husband had an honorary post at our embassy in Paris, and we stayed on. He died there just as the revolution was starting. Maria didn't get in touch with me for several years." She sighed. "I'd never seen your father when it all began, he was about five and they were living in the country then, near Moscow. One day a band of revolutionary soldiers arrived to requisition horses. Being pro-revolutionary, my father had no objection to handing over his horses. But the soldiers either thought his acquiescence suspect or were drunk — whatever the reason, they shot him, began to loot, then suddenly vanished without either explanations or horses."

From documentary films and recorded songs, I could visualise the pale wooden house, isolated among white-trunked birch trees and poppy-scattered wheat. I could see the door torn from its hinges, the deserted seesaw in the garden, the open windows that gave the place a sightless look; I could hear the raucous shouts, the outbursts of temper and laughter, the unpremeditated shots turning a live body into worms' food. That my grandfather had been murdered by accident seemed to me to make his end even more nauseating than if principles had been involved. My face grew hot, and I shivered with rage.

"What about Maria and the baby?"

"She was heartbroken. She'd loved her husband,"

continued Aunt Natasha, "but might have got over his loss. She'd loved the revolution in theory, but might have got over loving it less in fact. What she could not get over was the double loss. So, all her energy went to getting Vadim — your father —and herself out of Russia. She couldn't lay her hands on much money, in Berlin she washed dishes in restaurants to earn the fare to Italy. San Remo was her goal. There was still a large Russian colony there, mostly people who had removed their money from Russia before the war, let alone before the revolution. One of these, a princess who could barely speak Russian, but was now more royalist than the czar, gave your grandmother a job as companion to her children. She was determined they should have what she called a 'real Russian upbringing.' Vadim was allowed to share this 'upbringing' among icons, fabergé trinkets, and floridly framed royal photographs, attending the Russian church, and playing with other Russian children in similar circumstances. Nothing whatever was done to prepare them for the world in which they would presently have to earn a living. And it was there that I saw him for the first time."

"What was he like?" I asked avidly. I knew very little about my parents, and had believed they had been killed young, in a rail smash.

"A very pretty frail-looking blond boy in a sailor suit. Far less frail than he looked, and with an agreeably sinister sense of the comic. I took a great liking to him, and a great dislike to the way he was being raised. My husband suggested - "

"But - I thought he'd died, your husband, in Paris?"

"He had, God rest his soul. This was my second husband."

"The general?"

"The general."

"But Boris?"

"By that time Boris and I hadn't been able to get in touch with each other for years."

"Did you marry the general because you were desperate?"

"Desperately in love with him, yes." She sighed, then laughed. "He was such a funny man, most unsuited to generalship, but of course he's ceased exercising his functions when I met him."

"What was he doing?"

"Teaching Oriental languages, in Paris. We met in a second hand book in the Passage de l'Opéra. I remember it well because he was humming '*C'est le mois de Vénus.*' Out of tune and out of character. I think those covered passageways in Paris reminded him of the passages near the Kremlin – in the great bazaar that used to be to the left of the Tartar quarter. He was very interested in Buddhism and wanted to go to China. He thought your father might join us. He felt the future lay in the Orient. But it was useless to reason with your grandmother. Luckily for your father, she quarrelled with the princess when he was eleven, after which she became gouvernante in an hotel there, and Vadim was sent to a good Italian school and became for all practical purposes, Italian. Oh, what a darling he was. Far dearer to me than any other member of my family, except Yakov. I felt as if he were my son. As he grew up, he had a wonderful capacity for not judging people, for accepting them as they were – perhaps because his mother saw even her smallest dealings with people as trials of strength; oh what an exhausting woman she became, poor dear soul."

"Did you see them often?"

"Not very. The world is a small place only for people with big incomes. Next time I went to Italy it was to see Vadim married."

"Oh! What was my mother like?"

"You're very like her."

"Was she Russian too?"

"No, Italian. Well, French really. Her grandparents had been exiled from France after the Commune, and they'd settled in Pisa. Your parents thought of themselves as Italians."

"And that's where I come in…but then - I was born a refugee." Suddenly I remembered Anna of the delicatessen store crying out *I always thought refugees were other people.* "It doesn't say on my papers that I was born in Italy. Did they have to move on again?"

Aunt Natasha shook her head. "It was you that moved on, my darling, after they were dead-"

"Did they have natural deaths?"

Stretching out her hand, Aunt Natasha touched my face, running her forefinger over the bones' outlines. A wave of useless longing swept over me. My parents were gone, and no matter how much I loved Aunt Natasha I could never have as a companion the young girl she had been; I had come too late. "I do love you," I said, squeezing her hand and trying to thank her in kisses.

"Natural is such an ambiguous word, my pet," she said softly. "I suppose your mother's death was natural — childbirth."

"Of me?"

Aunt Natasha nodded.

"What happened to my father?"

"His misery took the forms of guilt, mysticism, of feelings that made him ill because his mind repudiated them. He became less and less capable of thinking what he was doing, or where he was going. In the end he was knocked down by, of all things, a tram. Here . . ."

Aunt Natasha dipped into a pocket and handed me a piece of bread, crumbs of wool clinging fluffily to it. I could taste tears and wool as well as bread, but the act of swallowing quieted me. "How did I get to you?" I asked.

"Your parents' lawyer, Spiro, arranged things. I had told him to get in touch with me in case of trouble. I wasn't going to have you in an institution. We could still travel then, you see."

"Wasn't it wartime?"

"The brink only. I got you home just before the Germans took us over. When that happened, Boris and I thought you had better have false papers."

"Then - I'm really Italian?"

"Really? Well, no. Technically you were, but really you're a quarter Russian, a quarter Czech, a quarter

85

French, and a quarter Italian."

"No wonder you thought false papers were indicated."

"It wasn't so much that as the fact that your parents came under the heading intellectuals — and Vittoria, your mother, was half Jewish."

Anti-Semitism was often discussed at school. Most people were against it, at least in theory. Reading about the war I had pitied Jews. Those poor people, I had said, seeing the star of David stamped into their flesh. Now they were no longer they. They had become we. For the first time I wondered why self-pity was generally deplored. It had been permissible for me to pity them as them. Why was it wrong for me to pity us? The situation was not radically changed by my participation in it. I understood now why Aunt Natasha had not spoken of this before. At home everyone has a police record, half of it secret, composed of other people's denunciations, the other half a four-page questionnaire one fills in oneself or has filled in by one's owner in the case of a child; and the most important part of this questionnaire concerns one's origins: for example, artists are permissible, but teachers suspect, as are peasants if they ever owned more than twelve acres.

"It was better for you not to know you had anything to hide," said Aunt Natasha, and although she didn't need to make any effort on my behalf, her voice was crumbling with tact.

I nodded, unable to speak as I thought of the care with which she had protected me, the skill with which she had seemed to tell me all our past while concealing so much.

"Could we ever prove I'm me if we wanted to?" I asked.

"Your birth must have been registered at Pisa, though there's been a lot of bombing there since. But if Spiro's alive . . ."

"Aunt Natasha, would you have told me this, if all this hadn't happened?"

"Perhaps. Later. I can't say for certain. It would have depended on what else was happening."

"But, Aunt Natasha—"

"What, duck?"

"You were still in Paris. What had happened to get you here — at home,... I mean there — by the time you took me over?"

"An accident. One day I came out of that theatre in the Champs Elysées where the Pitoeffs had just started acting, and jumped into a taxi. The driver kept craning round to look at me, but I took this as a tribute to my new hat, a cloche it was, all little blue-green feathers, how I loved it — never let anyone tell you, my pet, that there are better clothes than in Paris."

"I won't," I said, my throat tightening as I thought of evenings at home when Aunt Natasha had sat by the window, fiddling with odd bits of stuff that "might do for a blouse," and occasionally looking over her spectacles at the street in which the only pretty sight was the lilac.

"Then suddenly, halfway down the Avenue du Bois

— such a handsome avenue, smells of forests, and has a pink palace in it — suddenly the driver turned round and said in Russian, 'So you are going to the Yusupovs, princess?' and he stopped the taxi and it turned out that he had been a friend of my brother Yakov, so long ago it seemed, and we embraced and both sobbed a little and he told me what had happened to him."

"Yakov?"

"That I knew. Yakov was killed in the war. Presently I discovered the driver knew Boris too – and that what had happened to him was not altogether unlike what had happened to your grandmother. Generosity and common sense had made him pro-revolutionary. But once the revolution was under way, this same generosity proved fatal to him. Apart from anything else it made it impossible for him to believe in the infallibility of dogma. Always he saw the individual case. So of course he was arrested. And would have been shot but for the kind of muddle that so often occurs when revolution and bureaucracy combine, and even murder cannot be committed without a stamped paper in triplicate. The wrong ammunition was distributed to the men supposed to execute Boris. And during the delay he escaped, thanks to a warder who had previously been a poacher, and got across the frontier to the nearest republic, where he found a job with a circus. Once I knew where he was, of course, I had to join him."

"How could you afford such a long journey?"

"I still had a few things I could sell. His father, Anton, once gave me a couple of pictures by Renoir. Anton had paid about five thousand francs for them, but by this time they were worth eighty thousand." She sighed. "Though I was sorry to part with them. The people in Renoir's pictures always seem to be having such a delicious time."

"Wouldn't it have been better for Boris to come to Paris?"

"He didn't want to. He wanted to be near home, so as to cross nip across the frontier if things changed. He always meant to go back. For years we lived as if in a station waiting room. In a way we still do. Though we know now that that particular train's never going to come."

"But…did you want to go back?"

"No. I loved what I'd seen outside. And I didn't want to be tied to any place. In a way I think I resented having to like a country just because I was born in it. I liked what I'd chosen. But most of all I liked Boris."

"Yet you were happy with the general?"

"Yes…" she laughed, then sighed. "Oh dear, how sad that one can't pass experience on. You're certainly not one of those little crocodiles who think no one over twenty-five can feel anything, but how can you possibly understand that it's true Boris and I have preferred each other to anyone else (except you, my darling, in my case, and Boris's son in his, but that's different) nearly all our now long lives, but also true that during the eight – no," she counted on her fingers, "during the nine and a half years we were without news of each other, supposed each other dead, our lives were not filled by regret and

89

longing to the exclusion of the most energetic feelings for other people."

"I think I can understand," I said slowly, feeling somewhat as I had that morning, looking in the delicatessen window, enchanted by abundance. For a second I had an idiotic conviction that everything was going to turn out well for us.

"Listen - "

From nearby came the rattle of plates. All round the room talk subsided, like gas fires popping out. Sitting there, I thought of my parents in the land where the orange tree grows, of Aunt Natasha in a cloche hat of blue-green feathers, of a taxi driver carrying news of Boris across Europe to a pink palace. I suddenly saw a picture of something that had happened to me at school. I was in the cloakroom, looking for my skating boots, when all at once Ladislaus, who wasn't in my grade and had at that time not spoken to me more than twice, came up behind me, put his hands on my shoulders, swung me round, and kissed me. At first I was angry, partly because I hate being taken by surprise, partly because Ladislaus obviously expected me to be flattered. Then he kissed me again, and although still annoyed, I was less so, and thought more of the kiss than of the situation, and then my annoyance melted into a new, an exquisite sensation that made me tremble and enjoy trembling. For several days afterward I longed to re-experience this sensation and, at first, was able to do so merely by remembering this kiss. But, perhaps because I employed it too often, this method soon lost its efficacy, and I began wanting other kisses, not from Ladislaus, yet I didn't know from whom.

I won a chess championship — this and geometry were the only school subjects at which I always did well — and soon forgot those few days of feverish longings. I hadn't thought about them since, until now, when in a way I could not account for, they helped me understand Aunt Natasha's story.

After we had drunk our soup, and I had told Aunt Natasha to finish the schnapps because she felt cold and the floor was draughty, we made ourselves comfortable and slept.

The snore-filled room was still dark when I awoke, but the skylight had turned from black to grey. As I grew accustomed to the heaving sea of sleep around me, I realized that Aunt Natasha was breathing with a peculiar, light creakiness. I sat up and leaned over her. Her forehead was hot and dry, and she moved restlessly, as if trying to shake off a weight.

For a second I sat still, my arms pressed over my stomach. My heart was thumping. Then I got up and crept out of the room to look for help: to look for people who weren't strangers here themselves.

CHAPTER SIX

In the passage, light the colour of dishwater trickled over scuffed dark green linoleum and blistered brown hot water pipes. Opposite frosted windows hung engraving after dusky engraving of ostentatiously helmeted men killing each other with much display of muscle.

At the end of the passage was a draughty landing with half a dozen doors around it. Opening and shutting these I caught glimpses of a blackboard, test tubes, a huddle of blind-eyed plaster casts. Frantic at discovering no one in any of these rooms, I didn't reflect that it would have been very odd if there *had* been anyone there at this hour. Running now, I decided to search outside. Then, in the entrance hall, between two large baize-covered notice boards, I spied a door marked "Porter." I knocked, got no reply, turned the handle, and kept on rattling, muttering angrily to myself, "What are they paid for?" Just like an official. "Oh, hurry, blast you, hurry, hurry, hurry." After what seemed a very long time, light appeared behind the curtained glass upper half of the door, and presently the curtain was pulled back by an elderly man in pajamas, his eyes bleary with interrupted sleep. Glad to disperse some of my fear by blaming a stranger, I immediately began to grumble. At home I should have thought twice before doing this, and part of me, aware of the fact, was torn between self-dislike and admiration for the accuracy of Aunt Natasha's remarks about what being a refugee does to you.

Instead of retaliating, the porter patted my shoulders, first one, then the other, as if anxious to be fair to both. Then he tugged a uniform jacket over his pajamas, put a peaked cap over his few but tousled hairs, sat down at a rep-covered table, motioned me to do the same, and drew the two-piece telephone toward him. While telephoning, which he did very cautiously, handling the instrument as if it might at any minute turn nasty, he fumbled with his left hand at a table drawer and extracted a tin with grey and pink parrots printed on its lid. Pushing this across the table to me, he whispered, "Eat – go on, eat please." The tin contained gingerbread animals. As if worried by my hesitation, the porter drew back the tin, fingered various animals, and at last selected a gingerbread giraffe and handed it to me, laughing as people do to encourage a small child. Then he repeated "Eat," so anxiously that I began to cram myself with gingerbread animals. They were so stale and dusty that I felt I might choke if I went on eating them; yet the porter seemed to attach so much importance to my doing so that I feared my stopping might interfere with his telephoning.

At last, when he laid down the receiver, he wiped his forehead and said, "Thank God, the ambulance will come. Perhaps it would be best to have the poor lady waiting here." Shuffling in carpet slippers he opened a cupboard at the back of the room, tossed aside some flowerpots and half a dozen mousetraps, and produced a deck chair and an army blanket, with which we improvised a stretcher.

Daylight was seeping into the gymnasium by the time we crept back. But no one stirred. When we lifted Aunt Natasha onto the chair she only muttered in an odd, soft, clucking way, like birds' talk. She was very flushed over the cheekbones, but I thought the empty schnapps bottle might account for that. We got her out without disturbing anyone except the dogs, who pattered across the room, their toenails making clipping sounds on the floor. But after a few inquisitive sniffs they wandered back to their owners and lay down with a deep sigh, their noses pointing along their forepaws.

While we waited for the ambulance, the porter told me his name was Horst, that we were all in the Lord's hands, but that this was no reason for not helping each other. Which didn't prevent my worrying as to whether or not he would tell his syndicate what had happened. To my surprise he said he didn't belong to a syndicate. He had this job because he was a veteran. I wondered if Boris would count as a veteran. This was when I began wondering if we three couldn't find ourselves a porter's lodge here, for a start.

Now and again Horst looked anxiously from Aunt Natasha to the biscuit tin and back again, as if wishing she too might benefit from a mouthful of stale gingerbread. To distract him, I pointed to the picture on the lid and told him we had once owned a parrot just like one of those. This was not true but Horst looked so pleased that I was glad I'd invented it. By the way he spoke of them, parrots seemed to be an object of passion to him; Half listening to him, I thought with a pang that Aunt Natasha would have relished the idea of bright parrots flying through our darkness.

Just then an engine stopped outside, and ten minutes later Aunt Natasha was in the ambulance, and Horst helped me climb after her. I begged him to look out for Boris and tell him where we were, and he reminded me to remember, should I forget his name, that he was Herr Chief Night Porter at the Empress Elizabeth Gymnasium. Then we were off, the ambulance bell scattering its shrill cries of disaster. Leaning over Aunt Natasha I saw illness, visible as a mask now, beginning to veil her face.

At the hospital she was taken through a door marked "Emergencies," and a young man in a white overall led me round the building into a hall with a checkerboard floor of black-and-white marble. Across it, at a large desk, sat an older man in a white overall. My escort went and spoke to him in a low voice. The older man looked annoyed. An argument seemed to be under way. The older man shrugged his shoulders, took off his horn-rimmed spectacles, wiped them with a piece of yellow leather, and beckoned to me. "Good morning." He cleared his throat as if I were an audience. "I take it you have your mother's identity papers?"

For a second I stared at him. Of course I hadn't my mother's papers; but equally impossible demands have to be met every day. Then the young man said, "Probably her mother has them on her," and I realized they meant Aunt Natasha. I also realized that, as we kept important papers locked in the tea caddy that once be-

95

longed to Olga Knipper, and as this tea caddy had almost certainly been burned along with the rest of our belongings, we could therefore say anything we liked about our identity without anyone being able to prove here and now that we were lying. For a second I had an exhilarating sensation of freedom, including freedom to fool these two men. Shaking my head regretfully, I said, "I'm afraid our papers were left behind." As they looked put out, I added "The street was on fire…"

The man behind the desk shook his head and muttered something that included the words "Slav fecklessness." The younger one looked outraged, saying, "Oh really, for God's sake, and in any case they aren't Slavs."

At last, tired of bickering, they asked our names and home address. They asked our names and home address. I gave Aunt Natasha's maiden name, thinking that if we had the same surname no one could doubt our being blood relations or deny me the right to visit her in the hospital. They also wanted to know when we had arrived, by which route, and if there had been any incidents at the frontier. When the man behind the desk had written all this down in triplicate, I asked in a propitiatory tone if I might join my mother.

Immediately, they resumed bickering, the one behind the desk saying that strictly speaking this was not a visiting hour, and the other making explosive noises and asking why speak strictly, for God's sake. That was all very well said the other one, in the tone people so often adopt when meaning the opposite, and a good heart's an excellent thing, but there's a time and a place for everything, and what would happen if everyone indulged in heart? "This sort of thing wouldn't happen for God's sake," said the young man. Sighing as if much put upon, the character behind the desk said that the fact we lived in tragic times was no reason for blasphemy, and the other said, that was just where he was mistaken, and they glared at each other, like two dogs approaching the same lamppost from different sides. My anxiety to be with Aunt Natasha was so violent that I hated my friend as much as my foe. I was longing to knock their close-cropped heads together, when the latter mopped his protuberant eyebrows and said all right, all right, but if the Herr Direcktor found out and objected he refused to accept responsibility, was that quite clear?

Taking me by the elbow, the friendly one of them led me to an elevator. Not only did it work – when a button was pressed it glided swiftly upwards without a sound – but it had rubbery stuff, thick and soft as a good carpet, on the floor. Next, we walked down a clean white-walled passage with numbered doors on one side, and on the other windows overlooking a park. At the corner we met a pretty young nurse in a starched cap and apron.

When my companion asked about Aunt Natasha, this nurse gave me a glance, dubious but amiable, and said that, as there had been no room in the appropriate ward, the patient had been put in a private room just vacated by an appendix case. She called my champion "doctor" and obviously liked him. Looking relieved, he told her I was the patient's daughter, that the circumstances were unusual — here he paused, then said "refugees" in a hasty ashamed tone — so although he wasn't, of course, asking her to break regulations, he did wish she would look after me. The nurse said of course, I could wait in her room until my mother was ready for me.

Her room was extremely elegant: white walls, un-cracked ceiling, basin with running hot and cold wa-ter, shiny linoleum, bed with clean sheets and blankets, white chest of drawers, two cane chairs, and a desk. The nurse told me to try and relax, to wash if I felt like it, by all means to use her brush and comb, and she would be back presently.

When she'd gone, I examined the room. On the desk was a photograph of a plump smiling middle-aged cou-ple and, tucked into the frame, a snapshot of a young man, whom I recognized as the doctor, in white shirt and shorts, carrying a tennis racket. This cheered me. The toughest people can be induced to break regula-tions when in love. On the wall by the bed hung an ebony cross with a sprig of box tucked behind it. On top of the desk two wooden antelopes acted as book ends for a nursing manual, a breviary, a biography of Marie Antoinette, some poems by Rilke, and a book of coloured plates of Alpine flowers. There were also half a dozen illustrated papers with cover pictures of Maria Schell and Romy Schneider.

Going to the basin, I saw myself in the glass. My face was pale and grubby, and my hair, which I'd grown in preparation for the permanent wave, looked untidy and worn out. Having found a pair of scissors, I very carefully gave myself a pudding basin cut, then put the cast off hair in the bottom of the paper basket, and washed. The soap smelt of lavender and lathered foamily. I now looked as if I could get past most people without attracting notice — as was presently confirmed by the tone in which the nurse said, "That's better," trying not to sound surprised. But instead of leading the way to Aunt Natasha, she sat down and asked my name, which she had already been told.

"I'm afraid your mother won't be up and about for a while. She's tired, of course, after all you've been through. By the way, as you haven't any papers, could you tell me her age? It would be a help medically."

Fear pinched at me. Could they prove Aunt Natasha was too old to be my mother? Surely not. I had heard of women having children in their late forties. But in the interests of safety, I explained that she looked older than she was: had been through a good deal.

"Is there no one else with you?"

Unprepared for this question, I hesitated. I didn't want to deny Boris or make it difficult for him to gain admission to Aunt Natasha when he turned up, as I didn't doubt he would; on the other hand, I could see the nurse was already sorry for me, and I knew I must make her even sorrier and therefore likelier to break rules in our favour. Looking her straight in the eyes to show I was speaking the truth, I said, "My father's dead, and there's no one else except my uncle Boris. We couldn't find him — leaving so hurriedly — but he's sure to turn up."

"I see." She was clearly so moved by our plight that I fancied I'd better not embellish it. "Don't you think," she sounded apologetic, "you'd better stay with the other refugees? We'll let you know —"

"I want to stay here," I managed to croak, not acting now. "Suppose she needs me?" Suddenly I hated the nurse, the doctor, and the man behind the desk, hated the whole harassing world.

"Well, we'll see." She led me down several whitewashed passages hung with crosses and pictures of historical characters in halos, then put her finger to her lips and softly turned a doorknob.

There was Aunt Natasha, sleeping in a high white bed. She was still flushed over the cheekbones, and her breathing was very light and quick. A blank temperature chart was fastened to the bottom of the bed. Controlling myself, so the nurse would think I could be trusted here, I asked, "What is the matter with her?" The nurse looked at me thoughtfully, then said, "Pleurisy." A wave of relief swept over me. Aunt Natasha had had pleurisy before, and Boris and I managed to nurse her through it, despite a cold winter and inadequate heating. So she was bound to recover quickly in a place like this.

"May I sit here awhile?" I asked, wishing the nurse would go away. She frowned, looked at her watch, then said, "Just for a little while. I'll come and fetch you before the doctor starts his rounds." She looked so uneasy that I resented this, thinking "What's she got to worry about?" – which is nearly always a stupid if not a wicked thought – I pulled myself together and said, "If anyone should come in I'd say I slipped in without asking permission." Putting her hand on my shoulder, she said, "Do try and relax." This seemed to me a futile suggestion, so I said nothing.

After the nurse had left the room, I knelt by the bed and laid my head against Aunt Natasha. Her breathing was lighter than dried leaves skittering in the wind, and now and then she gave a harsh little cough. I was so frightened I couldn't hold my tears; but I managed to keep quiet except for my breathing, which sounded gross in comparison with hers. Then I closed my eyes and clenched my teeth and hands and tried, until my ears tingled from the effort, to will all the love in my body out and into hers.

CHAPTER SEVEN

When the nurse told me to leave, I knew it would be useless to resist. Also, I couldn't have spoken just then, and needed privacy in which to finish crying. My tears were becoming uncontrollable, and I was afraid of attracting notice by crying in the street. Luckily there was a dark corner two passages away.

I was still crouched there, vaguely aware of distant footsteps, of doors being opened and shut, of a gust of music from a radio, and of a newly diffused smell of roast meat, when someone tapped past on high heels, stopped abruptly, came back, hesitated, and a clear voice said, speaking German with a foreign accent, "Is something the matter?" Then added, what I was thinking: "Oh dear, what a stupid question. You'd scarcely be here if there weren't."

As she stepped nearer, I saw that the voice's owner was tall and slender, about Aunt Natasha's build, and held the prettiest, cleanest curling white hair I had ever seen. As her skin was soft and smooth, this white hair didn't make her look old, but did make it difficult for me to guess her age. She wore a grey frock and coat, black hat, gloves, and bag, had three rows of pearls round her neck, and was accompanied by a faint sweet smell of scent, so I knew she must be rich. I'd never seen anyone dressed as well as this before outside a rare foreign film.

"Can I help you?" She spoke as if she really wanted to, unlikely as this seemed.

Wondering how to turn this incident to account, I heard myself say, "Would you let me walk with you to the exit, and if anyone speaks to you say I'm a relative? Because I ought not to be here now."

"Very well." She spoke briskly, as if she saw nothing unusual in my request, and immediately led me down the passage. Now that I had a protector. we met no one except a maid pushing a trolley of shining soup tureens. Their domed lids offered us contorted reflections of ourselves, like ones in fun-fair mirrors. Despite my clean face and neatened hair, I already looked as refugees do in newsreels.

Once we were outside, I thanked her, holding out my hand. But instead of shaking it, she held it between her hands and asked: "Where do you live, my dear?"

I pulled my hand away. For all I knew she might be an official in disguise. I had never before met an official who smelled delicious, but that might be part of the disguise. Resenting her, I named our billet.

"I see." She looked at me speculatively. "There must be something I can do . . . whom are you with?"

Grudgingly I said, "My mother's in this hospital…."

"I see." but she looked as if she didn't. "Let's get in the car. The street's not the best place for talking."

She led me to a small grey car and told me to sit beside the driver's seat. Just then, to my horror, a policeman came up, tapping his notebook with a pencil in a suggestive way and eying us with the mixture of distaste and satisfaction that suggests one has been caught in the act. But the woman beside me seemed unmoved, barely allowed him to mouth a phrase about parking, and produced papers at the sight of which the policeman touched his hat, bowed, smiled, and removed himself.

"How did you do that?" I asked distrustfully.

"UNESCO still has its uses."

"You're a foreigner?"

"Yes. Do policemen always alarm you, or just at the moment?"

"Always. Don't they you?"

"Not as much as they should. I started life in a country where they're supposed to be comparatively harmless."

"A long way off?"

"England."

"Are you a refugee too?"

She shook her head. I hadn't thought this very likely, since she owned a car. "What kind of car is this?"

"A Fiat."

"Is that a German car?"

"No, Italian."

"Have you just come from there?"

She nodded, smiling. Her eyes were blue and very brilliant, suggesting jewels or minerals; and she had a peculiarly captivating smile – it made one feel both that one was a little ridiculous, and that there was something seductive about being a little ridiculous. Because of that smile, I came out with "I was born there," then stopped, furious with myself for having revealed something, not even under duress.

After watching me for a second, she sighed, then said, "Listen, my child, is German your only foreign language?"

I admitted I could manage in French or English.

"Oh, well, that simplifies matters," she said in English. "Now, my dear, you look brimming with alarm and despondency, and no wonder. Shouldn't trust anyone an inch if I were in your place. So, I'll give you some data about myself, and you can decide if you feel like trusting me."

Her voice was higher in English than in German, and she spoke faster, in a kind of hilarious rush, so that although I understood the gist of what she said, I found keeping pace with her a strain. Every now and again she would single out one word for tremendous emphasis.

"I don't distrust you," I said carefully. "But," trying to sound interested rather than suspicious, "why do you want to help me?"

"Why not?" She looked genuinely surprised.

She looked at me in a way I couldn't interpret, then said less rattlingly, "Well I'm not that kind of stranger. I go in for a certain amount of good works, like most women of my age and type – partly because it's expected of me, partly because my life's been easy enough for such innate good nature as I started with to have had a chance to develop…also I have got quite a thing about the young…I mean as long as people still have more hopes than memories one can do something for them…I suppose it was the war that really started me on this. I had charge of some evacuees from England, people were moaning on about how frightful they were – if-you-give-them-baths-they'll-only-keep-coal-in-them, etc – of course they didn't know the meaning of leaving things as they would like to find them, or perhaps they did and that was just the trouble – but I liked them…of course I'm only trying to explain this to you because - "

"Because I'm young and a foreigner, so don't count." Having made this pointlessly boorish remark I flushed to the eyelids. I didn't know why I'd adopted that tone, but I did realise this was no time for perversity.

"Because you are young and a foreigner," she said unreproachfully.

"Yes well, so I was in Venice when all this started, attending some advance guard – in other words out of season – film festival with my son Joe. Joe's fanatical about films, but quite undiscriminatingly, thank God, just as ready to drag one to a romp with that delightful Marilyn Monroe as to one of those unspeakable intellectual documentaries with slow close-ups of oh so slowly moving combustion engines, if you know what I mean?"

About intellectual documentaries, I did.

"But the moment trouble started up here, Joe insisted he had to come and see for himself – the young are so fond of appointing themselves God's overseers aren't they? Awfully good of them, but a trifle wearing for parents. So, I thought I might as well come along too. Joe unfortunately has a friend here at the moment – if he's not already across the frontier. I say unfortunately because although he's a dear – apart from going by the inappropriate and repulsive name of Pip – the child works for a Yorkshire paper that invariably takes a decent line politically, so is equally invariably right out on its tiny ear with practically everyone. Whenever there's a crisis, there's Pip covering it – and Joe's old enough to follow him on the inadequate grounds that 'Pip said I could stick around.' So at this moment I'm sticking around as a no doubt useless deterrent. Besides, once we'd actually got here..." her voice rose, cracked slightly, "there was an old woman with a donkey..." She stopped, carefully removed a tear or two from her underlashes with her forefinger, and said crossly, "Unpardonable of me, I'm so sorry."

She seemed to think it presumptuous of herself to display emotion about the homeless in the presence of one of them. Later I discovered that this feeling for precedence played an influential part in her character, as did a liking for anarchists and individualists, both types against which we were often warned at school. When I discovered this, I began liking her. But that was later.

"Have you other children?" I asked, wondering how many of them there would be to contend with.

"One. A daughter, younger than Joe, about your age, who will be a charming creature if she ever gets around to thinking of anything but horses. You're probably blissfully ignorant of pony club mentality - "

"The only horses I know belong to a circus."

"Thank God...by the way, what's your name, my

dear."

I told her, adding, "I don't know yours."

"Ruiz. Kitty Ruiz. Won't you tell me a little about yourself?"

Remembering Aunt Natasha's advice never to tell a lie, but not to tell everyone the truth, I gave a censored account of myself. Ever since Mrs. Ruiz routed that policeman, the idea had been growing in me that she might be able to provide penicillin or other black market products, should Aunt Natasha need them. So, I described her symptoms in detail, ending with, "but the trouble is, she has no business in that hospital."

"Why ever not?"

"Because they're afraid we may bring infectious diseases. and in the second they don't want refugees mixed up with other people even when we're not physically infectious. They're going to set up a special quarantine camp for us."

"How do you know that?"

"Horst, the porter, told me."

"Well, but — how did your mother get into the hospital?"

"Because the girl who answers the emergency calls at the hospital is married to Horst's son. They combined it between them. And there was a nice doctor. And once she was there, ill," I stopped, misery rushing back over me. "Will it take her long to get over pleurisy there?"

"Possibly not. Now listen to me, my dear, there doesn't seem much point, all things considered, in your going back to that school. Yes," as I opened my mouth to interrupt, "we'll stop by and see your porter so that no hue and cry is raised. Then I suggest you come back to the hotel and stay with us for the time being. They can easily put a camp bed in our sitting room, and why sleep on the floor when a bed's available?"

I was so astonished by this offer that for a few seconds I said nothing. At home we are not allowed to accompany foreign visitors up to their hotel rooms. We may visit them in the lobby, under the porter's eyes, but not go upstairs. Misunderstanding my expression, Mrs. Ruiz said, "I assure you it will be all right. My papers are in order; no one will think I'm kidnapping you."

It hadn't occurred to me that anyone might kidnap me, since neither financial nor political benefit could be obtained by doing so; but it immediately struck me that kidnappers, like most people engaged in illegality, would be sure to have their papers in order.

"I must let Boris know."

"Who's he?"

I hesitated, not wanting to lessen the alone-in-the-world-ness of my situation in Mrs. Ruiz's eyes before making sure of the penicillin. "An old friend and neighbour who helped us get away. He's bound to turn up."

"Then he's bound to go to that school, and the porter will tell him where you are. Did you bring any luggage?"

"Boris brought some of the horses."

Mrs. Ruiz breathed deeply, then said, "Apart from horses were you able to snatch up a toothbrush?"

I shook my head. "We were out, you see, and the house being on fire..." a shudder ran over me, the kind that indicates a goose is flying over one's grave. Aunt Natasha and I had never liked our apartment for its own sake – its eternal smell of cabbage soup, its elevator that hardly ever worked, its janitor who must be propitiated because of his police connections – but it was the only home I could remember, and at the thought of its being a bomb site, the ugly scars not yet hidden by flowering weeds, I felt weak and angry, regretting objects to which I hadn't known I was attached: the dressmaking dummy, Olga Knipper's tea caddy, a little leather box with three bees stamped on it, and the pedal-controlled sewing machine that sometimes hiccupped. Aunt Natasha being ill made me seize every opportunity for anger.

Mrs. Ruiz stopped the car in front of a big hotel as full of lighted windows as a government building on a reception night. Although there were only a few drops of rain in the air, a large man in a frogged plum-coloured uniform held a large plum-coloured umbrella over us as we walked to the revolving door, which was set in motion for us by a small plum-coloured pageboy. Inside were a great stretch of thick, soft plum-coloured carpet, and waterdrop chandeliers.

While I looked around, Mrs. Ruiz was talking to an imposing individual in evening clothes. Presently he gave me three looks, one of suspicion, one of pity, and one of grudging approval, each less intense than the preceding one. Then he said "Certainly, madame, but certainly" in unctuous tones, and led us to an ornate elevator, flattening himself against the wall and waving us bravely on as if the entrance were narrow instead of wide enough for at least three ordinary-sized people to walk through it at once. Upstairs, too, the carpet was so thick that our walk down the passage would have been made in silence if the radiators hadn't been gurgling like hungry stomachs.

The sitting room into which we were shown was full of luxury: a large pneumatic-looking sofa, a low table of shining wood half covered by newspapers and magazines with glossy covers, a shallow black china bowl of anemones. The telephone was equipped with several buttons, a little picture beside each – a girl in a cap and apron carrying a tray, a man in evening dress carrying a coat on a hanger, and a man in a loose jacket carrying two suitcases. The window overlooked a wide street punctuated by trees and lighted lamps.

"Sit down, Resi," said Mrs. Ruiz, who had tossed off her hat and was carefully rubbing her head with the tips of her fingers, "and be comfortable.

"We'll have dinner up here. And you'd better have Joe's room."

"Won't he mind?"

"Mind? My dear, he'll be delighted." Again, I was aware of something unusually persuasive about Mrs. Ruiz. Unlikely as it sounded, I could not help believing, for that moment, that a foreigner still unaware of my existence would be delighted to find himself obliged to sleep on a camp bed because I had his room.

I also — and this impressed me more — had the use of his bathroom, the like of which I had never seen outside Elsa's magazines. I was still examining it, turning taps on and off and fingering the thick soft-ribbed paper on which men were requested to wipe their razors, when Mrs. Ruiz came in with a toothbrush, washrag, and cake of honeyed-smelling soap. She also brought a long white nightdress.

After I had bathed and dried myself on a thick towel, warm from having been spread over hot pipes, I got into Joe's bed, the most comfortable I had ever been in, and was brought a tray laid with rolls and butter, a wing of chicken, lettuce, oranges, and a decanter of red wine. While Mrs. Ruiz was out of the room I wrapped a buttered roll and part of the chicken in a lettuce leaf, and the lettuce in a piece of the razor paper, and put that under my pillow. They might give Aunt Natasha enough to eat in the hospital, but I had no guarantee they would.

Then I ate and drank with concentration. The rolls were wonderful, soft white ones, quite fresh, with caraway seeds scattered over their golden brown outsides; and there was plenty of butter arranged in smooth curls, like tiny rolled-up golden fish, on a cockleshell of splintered ice. I began to feel as if there were a glass wall between me and the events of the last twenty-four hours. I half expected to wake up at home and find I had been dreaming of Mrs. Ruiz, smiling beside me, and of Horst, with a flame-coloured parrot on his wrist.

CHAPTER EIGHT

Waking with a jolt next morning, I didn't immediately know where I was. The smoothness of the sheets, the softness of my nightdress, the shortness of my hair, all flurried me. Then, remembering, I groped my way to the window and pulled back the heavy curtain. The street lamps were out, and a pale grey dawn made the snow that had fallen in the night look as if dirty fingers had been at it. In the distance, bells chimed. Shivering, I crept into the bathroom and turned on a tap, very slightly so as not to make a noise. Then I dressed and sat down by the window and waited for Mrs. Ruiz to wake. Although achingly impatient, I knew it would be useless to try and reach the hospital unaided. I had no map, and the streets were empty. Nor could I consult the hotel men downstairs. They would presume I was up to no good and wake Mrs. Ruiz, thus driving her to refuse penicillin. Mrs. Ruiz had given me no reason to suppose her capricious, but anxiety was making me unfair. Aware of this, I told myself I didn't care. I wanted to hit out at something or someone, preferably both – all the more so because I knew I couldn't afford to do anything of the kind.

At last someone moved in the next room. Presently there was a soft tap on my door. "Up already, my dear child?" said Mrs. Ruiz. She had changed clothes, and her blue pullover made her eyes look even more brilliant and jewel-like. "Did you sleep well? Are you ready for breakfast? I've telephoned the hospital. They say your mother has had an easier night, and you can visit her this afternoon. What's the matter?"

"How could she have had an easier night? It was her first night there. They don't know what the night before was like for her."

"I expect that's just their way of saying she had a good night." Mrs. Ruiz put her hand on my shoulder for a second. "Let's have breakfast, and you must meet Joe."

In the sitting room a young man in dark-grey corduroy trousers, a grey sweater, and windbreaker left the newspaper and map spread on the low table in front of him and shook hands with me. Except for his eyes and smile, he was so unlike his mother as to appear of a different nationality. Although tall, he gave an impression of being stocky, and his smooth skin was almost as brown as his hair, so he seemed to be carved all in one piece and to be more solid than people with a wider range of colours.

"I'm so sorry you're having such a lousy time," he said. "I do hope we can help."

"Thank you very much." I was relieved at his speaking seriously. Having heard a good deal about the stress the English lay on humour, I had feared he might make jokes like the complicated ones in back numbers of Punch, which we had studied for Anglo-Saxon psychology one term at school.

Breakfast was even better than supper. We had big glasses of orange juice, at least three oranges per glass, and fluffy scrambled eggs with little sausages and crinkled twists of bacon, and hot toasted white bread and all the butter we wanted, and a great deal of coffee and hot milk and sugar. Determined to try to please them, so they would provide just such a breakfast for Aunt Natasha when she was better, I sat up straight, unclenched my hands, and prepared to answer unavoidable questions. But instead of prying, they offered me a choice of newspaper and then settled to their own, occasionally looking up to smile or pass a dish, and including me in the smiles and passings.

I was prolonging my last piece of toast when the telephone rang. Mrs. Ruiz waved her napkin at it and Joe answered, grimaced, and said, "Would you mind waiting a minute, I'll just see if she's still in her room. I know she was on her way out so—" then put his hand over the receiver and mouthed, "Hadn't you better? It's that woman again."

"What have I done to deserve this?" Mrs. Ruiz moaned softly.

"Married into officialdom, darling," said Joe and handed her the receiver, into which she trilled, "How are you, my dear? No! How simply frightful. . . ."

Putting down the receiver, Mrs. Ruiz said, "Oh dear, oh dear, now I shall have to go round to the embassy right away, and God knows when I shall be able to make my getaway."

"You daren't cross her?"

"Not today. Who knows what favours we may need? You'll look after Resi, won't you, Joe?"

I was going to say, "I can manage on my own," but

115

was brought up short by the knowledge that this was a lie of the useless variety. Looking back, it surprises me that I felt no embarrassment at being entirely dependent on the kindness of strangers. But I had always seen Aunt Natasha ready to share whatever she had and frequently called upon to put this readiness into action; and as the Ruizes owned a car, travelled, stayed in hotels, and neither pocketed lumps of sugar nor examined the prices on the menu before ordering food, their readiness to help others seemed to me at least as natural as the situation that made us require help. Above all, the Ruizes were not yet real to me, except as potential support for Aunt Natasha. I still assumed love to be exclusively beneficent, was still unaware of the fact that anxiety - sharpened love for one person - can make one deeply callous toward everyone else. Joe was near my own age, and my consideration was reserved for older people. So it did not occur to me to apologize for wasting his time when he said, after his mother had left, "How would it be if I were to show you something of the town until we go to the hospital?"

Before we started out, snow had begun to fall again, but lightly, flakes drifting sideways so gently that one could almost distinguish their individual shapes. Sometimes we were in taxis, sometimes on foot, once in a streetcar, where I was surprised to hear people talking loudly, obviously not afraid of eavesdroppers. At home no one talks loudly in streetcars. I began to understand why, traffic apart, it was noisier here than at home.

As snow accumulated on the iron grilles beneath

them, the bare-branched trees acquired the look of toy ones based on circles of white enamel. Presently the light changed. Where it had been dull grey, a light for muffled living behind double windows and padded doors, it became violet, electric. Ordinary sights, such as half a dozen worn donkeys laboriously trotting into an amusement park, appeared in that light, at that hour, to have dramatic significance. Between the stream of lorries, trucks, streetcars, taxis, motor scooters, bicycles, and scores of candy-coloured private automobiles, warmly hooded people tried to scurry on booted feet. Soldiers marched stolidly across parallel lines traced in the snow by trams. Children in scarlet caps threw snowballs across a vacant lot. Inside a dusky church transparent cups of light burned, like cherry-coloured flowers, their small flames trembling before a meekly smiling doll in tinsel.

Imperceptibly, I lost my sense of time, so that now I cannot remember how long we drove about, stopping here and there, Joe quietly telling me about what we saw, not seeming to expect comments, just plying me with diverse facts, as he and his mother had plied me with food, to keep me going. Before we reached the hospital, we found ourselves in a street blocked by a seething crowd. Several policemen were running towards it, their white truncheons uplifted, their white capes swinging stiffly out behind them. Alarmed, I asked Joe whose side they were on. But they weren't on any side. People were merely pushing each other around in an effort to peer inside a café where a film was being shot.

Joe spoke to one of the policemen, and a way was made for us. People stared gluttonously, as if we were part of the film.

At the hospital I started towards the back entrance, but Joe steered me towards the main one.

"It's all right. Mother called up and fixed things."

"Still…" I looked regretfully towards the back entrance.

"Better not, really. The more you keep the rules when it's feasible, the more leeway you have when you need to break them. No point in sticking one's neck out for the hell of it."

This made me trust Joe. So did the way he dealt with the man at the desk. Then he came upstairs with me, sat down on a bench in the passage outside Aunt Natasha's room, said, "Go ahead, Resi, take your time," and drew a book from his pocket.

It was no longer snowing now, and brightness came into the air, showing up the cleanliness of Aunt Natasha's fresh bedclothes. When I saw her looking so much better, I felt so happy I almost cried. There was a mountain on her temperature chart, but a valley beside it. She had only vague recollections of what had happened yesterday, and asked me anxiously if I had had enough to eat. I produced the chicken sandwich which I had saved from my supper and told her about the Ruizes. She questioned me eagerly, and for a little while it was as if we were back home, each describing to the other the kind of day she had had. I told her Boris was on the way, and also of a plan I had thought out in one of the churches, namely, that Mrs. Ruiz should help Aunt Natasha and Boris and me obtain working permits, and then we should try to find a vacant porter's lodge where we could take turns at portering while I learned typing and helped Aunt Natasha start dressmaking again and Boris looked for a circus job. She liked the sound of all this, and we discussed which part of town we should prefer, in the unlikely event of our having any choice. For although I had only a chaotic first impression of it, Aunt Natasha had once known this city well.

To my surprise and joy, Boris, who had been given my message by Horst only half an hour ago, was waiting downstairs in the entrance hall. With him was Ladislaus. When I introduced them to Joe, Boris beamed with delight. Like Aunt Natasha, he was always delighted if given half a chance to be. This made him comparatively easy to understand.

The only person who refused to contribute a mite of friendliness to the occasion was Ladislaus. He wore a hangdog expression and every now and again ran his hand over his chin as if searching for bristle where there was only down. I knew this gesture of his. He gave Joe antagonistic looks, Boris contemptuous, and me inquisitorial ones. In the past twenty-four hours he had acquired a peevish, grudging air. Boris was so relieved at Aunt Natasha's being better that he kept hugging me. Then, eager to celebrate, he suggested we should all go to a café.

No sooner were we seated than Ladislaus got up again, looking furious, and went and fetched a news-

119

paper. After talking about Aunt Natasha — and despite his almost uncontrollable excitement Boris did not once forget that she was now officially my mother — we started discussing our future. Joe thought Boris' circus experience should be exploited, and said he had an American friend with influence at Ringling's Circus, might this not be useful? This reminded Boris of something, and in his enthusiasm he brought his fist down on the table so heavily that cups and glasses rattled. He had been forgetting, he said, to give us the most important news of all: he had seen a Red Cross delegate who thought we might be able to get to America; after all, we were able-bodied. Boris referred to our able-bodiedness as if suddenly discovering rare, hitherto unsuspected merits in us. The account he then poured forth of prairies, cowboys, Coca-Cola, skyscrapers, glorious opportunities for all was not very plausible, but neither would the prospect of our sitting here, discussing going to America, have seemed plausible a few days ago. Suddenly all my fears returned, because some people, especially strangers, might say that Aunt Natasha was not all that able-bodied. In fact she was elderly, bronchially fragile, and given to drinking too much. The thought that Aunt Natasha and I might be separated against our will so appalled me that, hearing Boris dwell lovingly on the word "future," I burst out with, "America isn't the only place where the future can happen."

Immediately, as if he had been waiting for this, Ladislaus threw down his paper, all traces of bad temper gone from his face. "You see! That's just what I was saying to Boris! Why always look abroad for the future?" He made "abroad" sound like an obscene word. "The fact is we ought to be ashamed of ourselves. Because we have no business business here." His face was flushed.

"What are you talking about?" Involuntarily, I spoke in the cold, balloon-puncturing voice I use when confronted with violent feeling of a kind I am determined not to understand.

"You know what I mean."

"I don't." But Joe's voice was friendly.

"Oh, well, you." Ladislaus spoke so rudely that I longed to slap his face, which suddenly reminded me of posters and platforms. Then I remembered his defence of the hens, and the fact that his father was still back home, and I felt sorry for him – and annoyed with myself for letting this pity weaken my ramrod of anger. However genuinely one may dislike oneself, I suspect one always ends by disliking even more the person responsible for this.

A sorrowful look came over Boris' face. He put his gnarled hand on Ladislaus' thin one and said gently, "Keep your temper for when you may need it, my dear boy. Don't waste it on us."

"Well, we shouldn't have come," insisted Ladislaus, his voice rising. "The whole thing was a mistake."

"The fighting?" Joe did not sound at all friendly now.

"No, I did not mean the fighting," cried Ladislaus, gasping just as he does in philosophy classes when told to clarify. "I mean our being here — we oughtn't to have left."

121

I was still sorry for him, when he looked at Boris and added, "I'm not blaming anyone," in a magnanimous tone, which made me so furious on Boris' behalf that I snatched up the nearest glass and threw its contents in Ladislaus' face. A second's silence followed, during which I was invaded by remorse. Considering how little money we had, I ought not to have wasted Boris' beer. When Joe beckoned the waiter and ordered more beer, I had difficulty in not crying. Boris put his arm round me and offered Ladislaus a large grubby handkerchief patterned with horseshoes. It had been my name-day present to Boris years ago. Refusing this, Ladislaus wiped his face with the back of his hands, shaking them afterwards as if dealing with rivers rather than drops, and announcing, "You can do what you like — no doubt you're already sold to the Americans. "But you know as well as I do that it is our duty to go back and fight; after all, you can't make an omelet without breaking eggs."

"People aren't eggs," said Joe.

"What's it got to do with you?"

In tears of rage, Ladislaus rushed out of the café, trying to slam the door. Since it was a revolving one, he merely set up a whirring sound like that of a giant toy.

Looking as he did when one of his animals was ill, Boris got up, said wearily, "I'd better see to him," and followed Ladislaus out. But I sat on, hate churning in me. I felt Ladislaus had betrayed me by suggesting we go back, when he must have known as well as I did that we could not take a no longer young person who had just had pleurisy back to a burned-down apartment in a city with a housing shortage. It did not occur to me that, since she meant nothing to him, Ladislaus had merely forgotten Aunt Natasha's existence, and had it done so, this would have added to my fury. His anxiety on my behalf seemed to me ludicrous and importunate. A little vanity would have made me kinder to Ladislaus, but my vanity was not of that kind.

"I'm sick of hearing about the future," I fumed. But what I meant was, our future frightens me.

"I know." Joe put his hand over mine. "Let's think of the immediate present. You had a good sleep last night, so I dare say you don't want to go to bed early this evening?"

"No, I don't." All I wanted at that moment was for it to be tomorrow, and visiting hour at the hospital, and neither mountains nor valleys but only plains on Aunt Natasha's temperature chart.

"Then why don't you come to the opera with me? I've got two tickets."

"What about your mother?"

"She doesn't like opera."

"Really?"

"Yes. I know it sounds cockeyed, but it's true. She doesn't like bullfights either."

I nodded, not quite so grateful as I would have been half an hour earlier, but grateful enough to realize I had better make an effort to sing for my supper.

PART THREE

'Without the gang you're an orphan.'
ARTHUR LAURENTS and STEPHEN SONDHEIM, *West Side Story*

'At the bottom of the heart of every human being, from earliest infancy, until the grave, there is something that goes on indomitably expecting, in the teeth of all experience of crimes committed, endured or witnessed, that good and not evil will be done to him. It is this above all that is sacred in every human being...'
SIMONE WEIL, *La Personne et le Sacré*

CHAPTER NINE

Joe's opera house was even handsomer than the one back home, in the same red plush and airy gilt style, full of cupids with dimpled bottoms of the same consistency as the pink clouds among which they gambolled, shedding musical instruments.

I had been afraid we would be late, but in fact we were early. The performance started at nine, instead of at seven thirty as at home, and the programs weren't free. Almost everyone there was dressed richly. I stared at the women nearest me, noting the stuffs their frocks were made of, so as to be able to give Aunt Natasha details of texture and colour. Particularly impressive was an inflexible gold brocade, the surface alternately glittering and crusty. Its solid magnificence suggested upholstery and gave the woman inside it the look of an odalisque, of being more an object than a person. Aunt Natasha loved stuffs.

As my clothes weren't suitable for the opera here, Mrs. Ruiz had dressed me in a coat bought for her daughter. It was of dark blue cloth, the nap so delicate that it changed colour, very slightly, if one rubbed a finger over it. Planning to wear this to the hospital next day, I imagined Aunt Natasha's eager questions. Going to the theatre was our favourite treat: shop-window gazing is liable to become frustrating, but one can take away whatever one sees at the theatre.

When I told Joe I had never seen tonight's opera

127

before, he looked pleased and handed me a slippery, red-tasseled program in which I read that the poet Hugo von Hofmannsthal wrote the scenario of *Rosenkavalier* in three afternoons of February, 1909, then sent it to his friend, Richard Strauss, who was so captivated that he immediately began composing music for it.

"Now," said Joe, as the audience broke into excited applause. Sleek as a penguin in his evening clothes, the conductor was bowing from the waist. The house lights went out, and a deep rosy streak appeared along the bottom of the crimson curtain's sculptural folds, as if reflecting a fire in the orchestra pit. Then the tide of applause receded, the conductor's baton emerged from the fire, the overture started. A prickling sensation ran over my scalp.

The curtain went up on the Marschallin and Octavian in each other's arms. Almost immediately their tender smiles and amorous gestures, complementing the way they sang, splashing in the music as delightedly as birds in sunlit water, made their love seem exquisitely light. It was as if they shared not only a secret but a joke. Being a mezzo-soprano, Octavian was sung by a girl, but she was as fine an actress as a singer and gave her boyish movements an innocent, impetuous greed, an unreflecting instinct. She snatched kisses as a child snatches candy, yet was disarmingly ready to share their sweetness.

Suddenly, I was reminded of the kisses Ladislaus had given me among the drying cloaks and scattered rubbers, and it was as if something in me contracted, turned over. The sensation combined discomfort and pleasure, but more pleasure, so that I longed to recapture it. When the curtain fell on the first act, met by great waves of applause, Joe turned and asked, "Well?" I nodded, incapable of speech. Then, all at once, I was incapable of silence, oppressed by a physical need to talk, to laugh, to shout, to vent some of the feelings roused by the music.

"Do all English people love opera as much as you do?" I asked, noticing the unmasked pleasure on his face.

"In fact, yes, many do. But I'm not English. Only my mother."

"What's your father?"

"Mexican."

"Oh." That half the world lay between us made Joe seem nearer to me than before I had known this.

"My father's Spanish. But he fought in the Civil War, against Franco, so had to get out afterwards. He was in a refugee camp in France, tried to get to America, couldn't get a visa, and at the last minute got to Mexico, where my mother joined him."

"They were married before all that?" Ready for the first time to be aggressive on Mrs. Ruiz's behalf, I remembered Boris saying, years ago, with a heavy sigh, "There is only one form of underground that never lets up, no matter how often it's defeated, and that is private life: the greatest resistance movement of them all."

"Yes, in Perpignan. That's the place in France where the camp was. Mother had volunteered to help the

Spanish refugees."

I nodded, relieved at having at last found a logical explanation for Mrs. Ruiz's kindness to refugees. Today, looking back, I find it hard to understand why I kept wanting an explanation for this, except that when Aunt Natasha was ill, suspicion blighted all my thoughts.

During the second act, in which Octavian — white wig, white knee breeches, glittering sword — presented the silver rose, I began resenting Sophie. Although forewarned of the plot, I hoped irrationally to see Octavian faithful to his first love; oh, how I longed in those days for stability, how unwilling I was to admit its rarity, with what aching unreason I yearned for the static in a world too full of motion. Yet I was touched by the music that leapt like a fountain of quicksilver from the young lovers' encounter, so much so that self-reproach entered my voice when I told Joe that I found the Marschallin in every way more attractive than Sophie. Smiling, half agreeing, he added, "When you're young I guess it's probably a lot easier to go for someone older than yourself. Because with an older person, their past stirs your imagination, whereas with someone younger the past has got to be quite a bit one's own work."

"That would bring laziness into it," I said, interested and suddenly guiltily aware that it was laziness that had prevented my seeing the Ruizes other than as Aunt Natasha's potential protectors. Because I was excited by the music, I wanted to make up for this and, during the second intermission, I asked Joe what his mother had been doing at the hospital the day I met her there.

Visiting the sister of an Austrian servant they had had in Mexico, said Joe. What about Mexico? I said. How did I mean, what about it? Well, what was it like? Had he always lived there until now? No, said Joe, he was born and raised there, but had started traveling pretty young and had not been back for several years. They had come to Europe right after the war - his father was a Mexican delegate — and had travelled not only in Europe but all over. Joe had gone to school in England, but not for long; he wanted to learn languages, and his parents thought traveling more important than school, and anyway they all liked being together.

"Tell me what you saw," I begged, as we walked to and fro over the thick red carpet, under the diamond-dropping chandeliers. Hunger for the places Joe had seen was added to another hunger provoked by music. Imprecise thoughts of love stirred in me, and with them a new feeling of hopefulness. "Tomorrow" had temporarily ceased to be a threatening word.

Suddenly as talkative as I had been monosyllabic, I harassed Joe with questions, and although he smiled at these, he took them seriously, his imagination coming more than halfway to meet mine. He knew instinctively that right then I wanted to hear about places, not people, and he understood this, having been a place-lover himself since childhood.

First, he told me of his birthplace: the pure, eroded landscape, creamy yucca flowers rooted in white sand dunes, cottonwood trees pale gold against the lion-coloured mesa, adobe huts and skyscrapers, cactus harvesting and rocket testing, sombreros and Co-ca-Cola, uranium mines and Spanish missions. Out of his words rose baroque towers radiantly white in transparent desert air, mountains purpled by distance, a spreading elf-owl-haunted cactus forest dominated by the ribbed green arms of the saguaro, stiffly upraised, like a giant candelabrum. Crossing the frontier to the United States, he remembered a house where he had been shown a wallet containing a faded photograph of Modjeska and a lock of hair, a relic of love washed up by time in the Arizona desert. He spoke of the mortician's handless clock ticking over Sunset Boulevard, of the cable cars rushing people up the coloured canyons of San Francisco to see the Golden Gate.

Standing in a cave in China he had seen a crowd in blue trousers and padded blue jackets silently watching an American film, *Weekend in Washington*; in the front row a young Chinese actress slowly tossed a scarlet chiffon handkerchief, drenched in synthetic orange blossom scent, to and fro beneath her tiny nose. Watermelon gaped from the stalls of the flyblown, night-shirted, hoarse-voiced lanes of Cairo, and terrorists in striped pants carried brief cases beneath desiccated palm leaves. Between the rosy marble, the sweat-stained khaki, of Jerusalem's steep streets perpetually sneering camels climbed, bypassing the old city's Needle Eye gates and jostling blue-jeaned kibbutz workers who had laid aside their rifles for a few hours' amusement: the quick and the dead caught up among the tangled mythologies of ancient history.

Just as a composer will return to a motif, so Joe kept returning to Italy, speaking not only of its beauty — the painted past coming to light in the darkness of an Etruscan tomb, fountains flinging liquid fireworks across columned perspectives, the wild delicacy of a topiary garden — but of the people who live there, of their love of life. Even in sorrow, even in poverty, they treat life with affection; the opposite, added Joe, to his father's birthplace, where death got all the prizes.

Of course, Joe did not tell me all this in the course of one talk between two acts of music. But because this was the moment of my geographical awakening, I came to associate much that I acquired later with this moment when Joe's place names seemed to be rushing into me on the same tide as the music. The culminative effect was an active wanting on my part such as I'd never felt before, except in a negative form – wanting Aunt Natasha not to be ill or miserable. Although I didn't yet know what I wanted, this was the first completely new emotion I'd experienced since crossing the frontier, and it exhilarated me.

This exhilaration grew during the last act of *Rosenkavalier*. When the Marschallin gave up Octavian, her singing of *Hab' mir's gelobt, Ihn lieb zu haben in der richtigen Weis'* drew tears from me. I remembered Aunt Natasha closing the eyes of the young man with a camera, and the shock of realizing that, for all his apparent youth and strength, he would never open them again; and as I listened to the beautiful voice singing of renunciation, I caught a glimpse of the fact that saying good-bye to a kind of love I was only beginning to understand might seem a death in life. Had Aunt Natasha suffered in this way?

As we walked back to the hotel, the snow friable under our feet, I was languid with enjoyment and gratitude. For the first time I had an inkling of the fact that the Ruizes' kindness was disinterested and therefore above price; I began to wonder, idly but definitely, not only where they had been, but what they had done there, what they were like.

"What are you going to be, Joe?" I asked as we got into our hotel sitting room, where the table was laid with ham, tongue, cold chicken, green salad, a bottle of red wine, and a bowl of apples, oranges, and bananas. The sight of fruit still seemed to me miraculous, and I ran my forefinger over the surfaces, liking the difference between the rugosity of the thick orange skin, the taut silky smoothness of the apple, and the other smoothness, more like linoleum, of the butter-coloured bananas. I did not have to appropriate food here. Mrs. Ruiz had already sent a big basket of fruit to the hospital.

"A photographer."

"Oh. Do you aim to do heroic things?" I asked uneasily.

"God, no." Joe laughed, then stopped, looked at me, and added mildly, "I mean that. False modesty seems to me as cretinous as boasting. I genuinely do not aim at heroism. Never mind how people die, what I care about is how they avoid dying, how they survive, how they live. But of course I'm inconsistent. Military service seems to me insane - making people waste time peeling potatoes in some goddam barracks, when war will be a matter of pressing buttons, and once the entire world's radioactive, much good it will be anyone's trying to occupy anyone. Yet I'm crazy about war stories, like that one about those British officers who captured the German general in Crete."

"Maybe you just like seeing a general made a fool of," I said hopefully. "But what about people resisting, like your father in the Spanish war; don't you admire them?"

"Oh, sure. I certainly do. But he — they - were against, they were underdogs, one can always see the point of the against side. But unless the world aims to bomb itself out of existence, a majority of relatively sane people have got to be for. . . ."

"Is that why you want to be a photographer?"

"Gosh, no, I just – well if I'd lived a generation earlier I guess I might have wanted to be a painter. But right now photography does so much only painting used to be able to do. Take refugees, for instance – you can tell about them, write about them, wave statistics, but none of it sinks in, half the time. But a photograph sinks in all right. A photograph's not theoretical. A photograph's people." Suddenly Joe stopped, looked at me, asked,

"You can't remember the war, of course."

"Not much. Not that war, at least. You can't either, can you?"

"Not much. But nothing I've heard or read about it, nothing, not even Papa's stories about the Civil War, got me the way a book of photographs did. I saw it about ten years ago; I was still a kid. Photographs of a concentration camp. Piles of dead bodies, like a compost heap. Resi, do you think any idea's worth that?"

Slowly, I shook my head. "Except . . . perhaps . . . the idea that that sort of thing shouldn't ever be allowed to happen again."

"And maybe that's the most insidious of all. Years later, in New York, I met the photographer who had taken those pictures. He told me that while he was doing it he had to keep stopping to vomit. In one room, beside the ovens they shoved people into, was a whitewashed wall and, painted on it, the rear half of a wild boar, and astride it, the lower half of a man in riding breeches, and, printed alongside in Gothic letters, 'Cleanliness Is Next to Godliness—Don't Forget to Wash Your Hands.' Why, Resi - God, Resi, I'm sorry - why on earth did I have to go and talk about things like —"

"It's not that, Joe," I protested, fighting to get the better of a sudden dizziness. "In the end what else is there to talk about?" I was afraid I might be going to faint, which I had never yet done. "There's always that going on underneath, always someone torturing someone in a vicious circle. Early Christians get tortured; then later, Christians do the torturing. No matter what the label, there's always someone doing it, and nine times out of ten doing it on principle." I heard my voice climbing steeply, trying to escape into the world of light the music had opened to me a few hours ago. But it was no use. There was no escape from the something clawing its way to the surface of my mind. Shivering, I muttered, "It's not that."

"Can you tell me what it is?" Joe's arm was round my shoulders, holding me the way Boris holds a shivering horse.

"It was years ago; there, where the memorial tank is, only it wasn't the memorial tank then. Two huge trucks arrived, and all at once there was a crowd of women and children, crying out, and soldiers, and the sound of rifle butts on skulls. They were forcing the women into one truck and the children into the other, and then they drove them off in opposite directions."

A moment ago, I had not been conscious of remembering this. Now it was as vivid to me as if happening all over again. The wind made my ears ache, and I heard the controlled terror in Aunt Natasha's voice as she snatched me up into her arms and whispered, "Don't be frightened, baby, there's nothing to be frightened of, we're only running because we're hungry, there's soup for supper, and we'll soon be home." She held me tightly, pressing my face against her coat, which smelled and tasted like an old blanket.

"I can see why you'd rather be a photographer than a journalist," I said shakily, seeing the outstretched arms, the frantic blue finger tips. "But you've got a great friend who's a journalist, haven't you? Your mother was telling me."

"Yes." The name Joe mentioned was vaguely familiar.

"I thought his name was Pip."

"We call him that." Joe looked surprised. "Why?"

"Have you heard from him lately?"

"Pip never writes. Just turns up. Right now, he's due to turn up any minute. I'm surprised he's not over there already."

"He was." My hands clenched themselves.

"What do you mean? How do you know?"

"I saw him."

"You did? Where? When?"

"Back home. That morning."

"But why didn't you tell us -"

"I didn't know. Your mother said Pip. I only knew his real name. And you said a journalist. But he had a camera."

"Pip often takes his camera along, just in case. You spoke to him?"

I shook my head.

Joe stared at me, uneasiness spreading over his face, giving him a sallow look. His eyebrows drew together in a thick dark line of concentration.

Hunching my shoulders, I tried to think how best to tell Joe the news I could not prevent from hurting him. Then, abruptly, he asked me how it happened.

"I don't know, Joe. We were running down an empty street, away from a tank, and suddenly we saw a young man with a camera running in the opposite direction. He looked queer, I realize now; but at the time nothing did look queer, because everything was. Then suddenly he raised his arms, like the conductor tonight. And then he fell. Aunt Natasha and I ran to him. But it was too late. We looked at his papers. That's how I knew his name."

"Tears ran down Joe's face, and he swore again and again, softly and monotonously. Suddenly he stopped, stared at me, and asked, "Who's Aunt Natasha?"

My heart gave a sickening jolt. Then, kneeling beside him, I said, "Oh, Joe, I'm so sorry about Pip, so very sorry. I know that's no help, but I am. Aunt Natasha's my mother, I mean she isn't, but I said so at the hospital so I'd be her next of kin, and they'd let me in any time."

On and on I went, explaining Aunt Natasha and Boris, Uncle Matthias' caviar, old Nina and Ladislaus, Boris' horses, the shutters slamming overhead as we ran, the smell of petrol, the dreamy smile on the young man's face, the Skaters' Waltz, Anna of the delicatessen, the sight of fruit. It was the first time I had ever tried to describe our life truthfully to any outside person. Joe had regained control of himself, but his sullen, almost military look of grief made me angry with Pip. We were still sitting there, silent now, like two people who both have toothaches, so know that kind words will not alter the situation, yet slightly glad to be together, when the telephone rang.

CHAPTER TEN

Hardly aware of what he was doing, Joe fumbled for the receiver. Now the stiffness had left his face, he looked slightly drunk. "What?" He gave the receiver a little shake. Then he looked at me, seeing me this time, and nodded and said, "We'll be right over," into the telephone and, to me, "Your mother, I mean your aunt, wants to see you, Resi."

For a second we stared at each other, then both moved, equally fast. Joe helped me into my coat, tossed over gloves and purse, put on his own coat, scribbled a message for his mother and, at the door, turned back for a scarf, which he thrust around my neck. Then we ran to the elevator. Neither of us spoke. There seemed nothing to say. But Joe held my arm grimly, as if we were walking across a slippery surface and still had a long way to go. Downstairs, dwarfed by a potted plant, a bellhop was swallowing yawns. Outside, a taxi was just stopping. A man in a black coat and white scarf emerged and held his hand out to a woman in a gold brocade frock. I felt further from them than from the strangest savages in the most time-speckled documentary film. The driver had to go slowly. Now and again the taxi skidded on a rut of ice.

Red lights were burning over the hospital entrance, as they had burned over the theatre exits after the rest of the house lights were off. But I was back in a world where neither lights, carpets, curtains, nor elevators that work can camouflage the fact that nothing is too terrible to happen before one is shovelled into the ground and, no matter what does or does not happen, the final shovelling is inescapable. I asked Joe to fetch Boris.

Hurrying down night-lengthened passages, I gradually became aware of a steady humming, as if a giant bee were thinking aloud behind each numbered door. The nurse was outside Aunt Natasha's room, her hand on the knob. She had a smudged look of exhaustion. Turning the handle without a sound, she opened the door. A man in white overalls stood beside the cage of transparent shiny paper set up on the bed. Inside this lay Aunt Natasha, eyes shut, cheekbones flushed, and with a crumpled look that had not been there earlier. The nurse and doctor glanced first at me then at each other.

Now they were taking the oxygen tent away. Aunt Natasha's breathing was punctuated by small whistles, like those of a child longing, but not quite daring, to provoke chaos in a classroom. Then she opened her eyes. Her lips formed a crooked smile. "I could do with a little sip of something," she said, half as if she meant it, half in self-mockery. Instinctively, I looked around. On the under shelf of the bedside table stood the basket of fruit Mrs. Ruiz had given us. None of it had been eaten. Not even the pineapple, with which Aunt Natasha had been particularly delighted. My throat ached as it had done after I had my tonsils out. I touched her cheek. Although hot and dry, it felt softer than ever before, soft as a really old person's. Suddenly the emptiness inside me was filled by commotion. As if in a nightmare, every bit of me began silently screaming out against what I still would not admit was happening.

"You're going to be all right," I heard myself hoarsely whispering. "You are going to be all right, this is just the last lap, they wouldn't be spending all this money on you, and clean sheets again today, if you weren't going to get better, it's going to be all right about the working permits too, and the porter's lodge, I've got my eyes on just the one, we're going to do fine, the three of us."

She was still smiling at me, but fixedly, a long-distance smile. She had smiled that way once years ago at the railway station, seeing Boris off to join the circus on tour. We stood waving and, as the train moved, Boris leaned further and further out of the carriage window. For several minutes after we could no longer see him, Aunt Natasha kept right on waving, but more and more slowly, as if her arm were a piece of machinery running down, and she smiled just as she was smiling tonight. Now, at last, my words seemed to reach her. Her smile loosened. She focused me. "Nice . . . and warm here," she murmured between whistles.

"The porter's lodge I was telling you about has such a good heating system," I rushed on. "Even if it's a bad winter we'd be all right there. And food's a bit cheaper than at home, I've been checking on prices."

Nearby a door was opened and shut. Someone had been running. When Boris knelt by the opposite side of the bed I was appalled by the greenish pallor in the depths of his face. Emotion could not alter his brick-

and-leather tan, but his surface skin suddenly looked detachable from the rest of his face, like peeling wallpaper in a damp room. He managed to smile at Aunt Natasha, and she smiled back, and for a second, because we were all three together, we were in a lifeboat. Then Aunt Natasha's eyelids began fluttering. Kneeling closer, Boris and I willed her to stay alive, to fight back against whatever was trying to snatch her from us, from little sips and sordid worries, trivial treats and the power of love. Her concertina-like breathing was the only sound in the room.

Suddenly she opened her eyes and looked around. The crooked smile was still there, but instead of being behind it she seemed to have moved up, to be struggling to peer from behind her eyes, glittering now. "Darling," I whispered, "please, please." Recognition cleared her eyes for a second. She burrowed her head deeper into the pillow, gave a light sigh, as if of well-being, the kind of sigh I had often heard her give, glass in hand, when we were all three sitting in the kitchen at home, the heat working, something for supper, and no particular trouble in the offing. Then she turned her head, looked straight into Boris' eyes, laughed, and said, "Listen my darling love -"

The rest of the sentence was submerged by a sound like that of an engine refusing to start. Her hands fluttered, helplessly reaching for non-existent help. Her beautiful eyes were empty as a window from which someone had just stopped waving. Boris' head collapsed against his arms. In between sobs I heard the pipes gurgling. But there was a sound missing. I listened for it with maniacal attention. Then something seemed to explode in me. There was a scream. The screaming went on, hurting my head, and was followed by words: "Aunt Natasha, Aunt Natasha, no no no."

People came running. Doors banged. This sudden banging, unaccompanied by shushing, made me realize with my mind, as well as with my nerves, that Aunt Natasha was dead. Tears rushed down my face, a bead curtain between me and an unfamiliar nurse who was saying, "She's coming, dear, do try and - all right, dear, your aunt's right here." Abruptly, Boris and I stopped crying and jerked our heads round, staring at the nurse. Now that it was coming in gasps, our breathing replaced the sound Aunt Natasha had made. Insanely hoping we stared at the door.

When Mrs. Ruiz ran to me, followed by Joe, I cried out accusingly, "Why did she say Aunt Natasha was coming? Why —" but I couldn't say more. The nurse was telling Kitty Ruiz, "I'm afraid her mother…it's unhinged her, poor child, but she did ask for her aunt - for you."

Reminded that even the dead are not exempt from filling in forms, I stumbled round the bed, away from that basket of fruit, to Boris. He took me in his arms, pressing my cheek against his jacket with its familiar smell of stables. Grief shared is not grief halved, but we both tried to muffle our sobs. From force of habit, we did not want to wake Aunt Natasha.

PART FOUR

'…tous les êtres on tune aptitude à s'accommoder, et cette aptitude variable meure leaur aptitude à vivre, c'est-à-dire à demeurer ce qu'ils sont, en possèdant plus d'une manière d'être qu'ils sont.'
PAUL VALÉRY, *Variété*

CHAPTER ELEVEN

Side by side on a wooden bench, Boris and Ladislaus are waiting their turn in an office now being used as a refugee repatriation centre. An amnesty has been proclaimed. Once again, revolt has been quashed. Once again, haggard pedestrians trudge through corpse-littered streets and ask themselves why without even expecting an answer. This is fortunate, since they do not get one. The atmosphere is cold and foggy. It is easy to mistake anguish for apathy.

Before this, the office was a travel bureau. The posters on the walls offer music in Salzburg, cures in Baden-Baden, skiing in St. Moritz, the Colosseum in Rome, the Eiffel Tower in Paris, Horse Guards in London, bays in Naples and Rio de Janeiro — worlds that, so far as most people here are concerned, do not exist.

As I come in from the street with a gust of cold air, a small boy not yet inured to waiting manages to clamber up, tears down a bit of skyscraper, and thrusts it into his mouth. His mother promptly emerges from a fiercely whispered conversation with her neighbour and slaps the child. With a powerful shriek, he relinquishes the sodden fragment, and his nose begins to bleed. One or two women glance in his direction and say, "It's a shame," but perfunctorily. Though glad of an opportunity to be censorious, few of us have by this time any energy for minor shames.

At the prospect of struggling yet again to dissuade

Boris from going back, I feel very tired. Apart from an obscure conviction that officialdom will always play in our daily life the part moths play in closets, I still have remarkably few political ideas. My earlier anger at Ladislaus' attempt to drag us back was due not to any considered desire to change places, but to my determination that Aunt Natasha should convalesce with a roof over her head. This point no longer has to be considered.

Ladislaus does not dare utilize this fact. He is reluctantly but genuinely intimidated by my black clothes, with their strong but inoffensive neutral smell of stuff that has not yet needed cleaning. Alert for opportunities to be angry, I despise him for this. Everyone's motives seem to me suspect, except those of Boris, Kitty, and Joe; or it might be nearer the truth to say that I understand Boris' motives, and hardly think of Kitty and Joe as having any. For me, these two still live on the further side of an invisible frontier. This makes their company unexacting. Occasionally, Joe crosses this frontier, as when he and I turn the pages of an illustrated weekly containing photographs of and by Pip. New print smudges under our fingers. "He never made the front page before," says Joe savagely. "How they like you to be dead. Do anything for you then. The only infallible way to win friends and influence people."

It is Joe who insists on my being supplied with mourning. When first he speaks of this, Kitty looks distressed and says "Oh, why, darling, too young, Aunt Natasha surely wouldn't have wanted it." "That's not the point," says Joe, not waiting for my answer—I am still incapable of uttering more than a few words without bursting into tears — "The point is Resi. How's she to handle herself? She may not need mourning right now, not here where half the town's in mourning. But she's going someplace else eventually. And she's young enough for people to ask her cockeyed questions, hell bent on getting enthusiastic answers. 'Aren't you glad to be here?' That sort of crap. Which you don't ask a person in mourning, for God's sake." And a look of disgust comes over his face.

For this look of disgust I am at present more positively grateful to Joe than for anything else. Like the severity with which his face meets grief, it reveals a capacity for impersonal irritation, that fragile but unique prop of justice. But the black clothes do have a keep-off-the-grass effect, and I am aware of this, even in the dazed state in which I move about, trying to cause no inconvenience except to officials, against whom I now feel malevolent impulses. I don't understand these impulses, nor do I try to, and they are encouraged by my conviction that I have nothing to lose. In my imagination there is an abyss between the deserted streets through which Aunt Natasha and I once ran, and the corpse-scattered, tank-congested, shell-gutted city in the newsreel I have just seen. This newsreel contains a shot in which a tank crashes into a kiosk where we used to buy newspapers. The tank pauses there, heaving, a bit of the kiosk caught up on its snout. Beside it, dead bodies lie like bolsters.

Remembering this, I vainly struggle not to understand that, having experienced so many changes, Boris feels unequal to more, unequal to getting acquainted with a place in which he and Aunt Natasha never lived together. If I no longer care about familial surroundings, it is because without Aunt Natasha there is, for me, no familiarity. But Boris is like those retreating soldiers who yearned for the condemned sleep in the snow. As it is comparatively difficult to achieve suicide, I envy him for being older that I am, nearer to nothingness. Yet, to my surprise, I am not short of arguments with which to attempt to keep him alive. That they are illogical escapes my notice. So are his in favour of returning.

As we start to argue, Ladislaus' face assumes a recently acquired look. Every inch a chieftain. The fact that his present decision concerns life and death instead of to keep or not to keep white mice ought to touch me, but doesn't. Not at the time. No emotions are simpler or more commonplace than those involved in losing the person one loves best in the world, but Grief has not ennobled me. Nor have I yet met anyone it has ennobled. This seems to me natural. Neither courage nor courtesy can alter the fact that grief is an amputator. So instead of making an effort to understand Ladislaus, I wish ferociously that he would remove himself. Presently he does just this, but takes his time about it, thrusting his hands into empty pockets with ostentation, in order to show that he is only going to the window because his legs need stretching.

Boris refers again to the amnesty. As we have known

other amnesties, his belief in its viability is as fragile as my own. But he speaks as if this were not so. There is something unnatural about the courtesy with which Boris and I attend to the other's views. We are overdoing it, on purpose. Each afraid the other may have lost the capacity to feel, we both deliberately manifest a type of consideration that would be superfluous were this the case. Then, seeing Ladislaus turn back to us, I say, "Well, but, Boris, amnesty or no amnesty, there's still fighting going on —"

"That's not official," he says this quite seriously.

"Still, you don't want —"

"I want to be somewhere familiar." When he speaks naturally, his voice is slurred by exhaustion. "I've nothing to lose, so I may as well lose it at home."

"Then I'll come too."

He shakes his head. "You'd only be in the way."

"You only say that because you think it's the only argument likely to have any effect on me, you know you do."

He smiles dejectedly, then says, "I know it doesn't seem so now, Resi, but you've got the future."

"The future?" An emotion I don't understand seizes me. "I hate the future," I cry, and at that moment this is true. "I hate the future. Ever since I can remember, everything dreadful's always been done because of the future, excused because of the future. One might as well be a Christian and shift everything onto the back of the afterlife. Oh, Boris, don't sound like Ladislaus. It isn't as if you can be consistent the way he is, he really thinks we owe it to the future to go back, but you wouldn't have gone back if Aunt Natasha were still alive, you know you wouldn't, oh, damn, damn, damn," because I am crying again. Not that this makes me conspicuous. Tears are commonplace in this former travel bureau.

"It's true." Boris puts his arm round me, gentling the anger out of my sobs. "It's true I wouldn't go back if she were alive. Not till she were well. And not unless she wanted to, even then. I couldn't do that to her again." A haggard look comes over his face, then he rubs the bridge of his nose and says, "I only meant that as long as you've someone to care for, you've got a future."

"I care for you, Boris," I say, meaning it, yet helplessly aware that I am offering him less than a shadow of what I gave to Aunt Natasha. With her, the world outside seemed to me unpredictable hostile; without her, I have no inside world, and my capacity for loving is diminished accordingly.

"So do I for you, Resi dear," says Boris, and I know he is up against the same difficulty.

"Ladislaus says -"

"To hell with Ladislaus."

My astonishment at Boris' tone shows me that I have never before heard him curse a personal acquaintance. Like Aunt Natasha, he tends to see three sides to every question, and has even been known to suggest that civil servants and policemen are human.

"If it's the last thing I do," he continues, glancing with uncharacteristic animosity toward the window, "if it's the last thing I do, I'm going to stop Ladislaus' ruining your life the way I ruined Natasha's."

"The way you —"

"The way I ruined Natasha's."

"But you loved her."

Sighing explosively, Boris runs his fingers through his already upended hair. "All the more reason. Listen, Resi, you may not think so, but I'm asking you something important."

"What?"

"You don't love him, do you?"

"Who?" Suddenly nervous, I am prepared to be on the defensive.

"Ladislaus."

"Ladislaus? Of course not." My scorn is genuine. I am still at an age to imagine that only certain categories of person are romantically lovable: the wicked perhaps, but not the dull. It has never occurred to me that I might love Ladislaus.

"In that case," says Boris with faint satisfaction, "there's no reason, no reason at all for you to pay attention to what he says. Because he'll go the way I went. You can take it from me. Despite the difference in upbringing, I know the type. I can see it all as clearly as I can see your wretched little white face…at the moment Ladilaus is wrought up, all ideals and self-sacrifice. But he's not only idealistic and fanatical, which sticks out at his age, he's potentially weak and affectionate – and when he finds himself at the liberty-what-crimes-are-committed-in-thy-name stage, he'll be stunned to discover you can no more make a robot out of the incalculable than you can catch the wind in a net. You'd have to go a long way to find a better specimen of the type made to be shot by both sides."

"But," I am greatly struck by this, "but, Boris, suppose that's the type I like?" As I say this I am convinced that for once Boris is wrong; Ladislaus is not at all like that.

"Then I'm going to try to make sure you like it someplace where liking it is feasible. You're not going to repeat Natasha's mistake."

"But she never said —"

"I don't suppose she did. I don't suppose she ever saw that situation the way it was."

"How was it?"

Boris runs his hand over his face, gnarled fingers separated by his handsome crooked nose, his eyes squinty with attention. "She was all right in Paris," he begins, and suddenly I know from his tone that he has argued this way, against himself, over and over. "More than all right. She wasn't pining. Not she. It wasn't in her character. She just had to love someone. Or rather, she just had to love. If a lamppost was all there was available, she loved that, and made a success of it." His voice is honeyed by the indulgence into which time has changed his jealousy. "There was nothing inevitable about it," he continues. "Nothing at all. There she was. There I was. And the length of a continent in between. She'd given up searching for me. So had I for her. What was the good? You can't defeat history. And that would have been that, if only she'd not run into that taxi driver."

"But, Boris, whether or not she was still looking for you, she wanted to find you. She told me so."

"Of course she did. So did I want to find her." A little ardour flickers in his face. Then he looks at me with tenderness and exasperation. My throat tightens. I sense that this tenderness and exasperation are intended not for me but for a young Natasha I can only guess at. Yet the expression is familiar. Someone else has recently looked at me in just this way.

"You'll understand when you fall in love." Boris speaks in a tone suitable to "when you have scarlet fever." "Of course we wanted each other. All the same, if want had been our master we'd have had to keep going where we were, at different ends of Europe, in different worlds. Not only that, but if I'd been somewhere a trifle more inaccessible than what was then a nice new old-style republic she couldn't have got to me and she might be alive now, alive and happy…There's only one thing I can do for her now: prevent you from making the same mistake without the excuse of love."

"If you go and I stay we shan't see each other again, and, Boris, we're all we've got."

Shaking his head, Boris puts his free hand under my chin and tilts my face toward him. "You make everything personal. Just like Natasha."

"Am I at all like her?"

"A little. But you have some of your grandmother's ruthlessness too. Maybe that will safeguard you against emotional improvidence."

Still inside the circle of Boris' arm, still looking at him, I slowly realize that I have already lost him. He is trying to protect me for Aunt Natasha's sake. I am doing the same for him. Equally ghost-ridden, there is nothing more we can do for each other. I shall never forget Boris. But here among the posters is our last station platform. Our smiles are fixed, our throats stiff. Now the past is over. And I don't want the future - then, suddenly, as if she were beside me, I hear Aunt Natasha say, "Nothing's ever over and done with, there are prolongations in time."

I am still shivering when Ladislaus strolls over and, eyeing us complacently, says, "So you've decided to come back with us after all?"

If there were either affection or anxiety in his voice, I would try once more to persuade Boris to take me along. But Ladislaus' manner is hectoring, his voice febrile, and he keeps looking over his shoulder. It does not occur to me that he is derailed among broken images and exhausted by his struggle to convince himself that this is not so. Instinctively, I want to do the opposite of whatever he advises. I don't want to share the future with Ladislaus, and suddenly I know that I shall forget him, forget him to such an extent that one day his name will escape me. As if sensing my thoughts, he exclaims angrily, "You're going to America! You are! Go on, admit it."

"Don't be a bloody fool," says Boris harshly. "Resi's going to —"

"Resi's going to choose," says a fourth voice. Joe has

just arrived to pick me up as arranged. Involved with Boris, I had forgotten this arrangement. But Ladislaus must have seen him crossing the square. Hence the backward looks.

"Yes. I don't have to" — suddenly it dawns on me — "right now I don't have to go anywhere." For the first time in my life, this is true.

Making this discovery, I am startled by Joe's expression. It is one I haven't seen on him before. He looks pale, furious, despairing. Something stirs in me. If Aunt Natasha were there to be told about it, this something would be identified as pleasure. But I'm on my own now. So, I don't understand my feelings, let alone anyone else's.

"I don't have to go behind curtains, nor across oceans," I say, slowly groping my way. "And it needn't be always the future. Not if I can choose. Because I can choose the present."

Tears come into my eyes. Looking at Boris, I again remember him calling private life the greatest resistance movement of them all. Ladislaus puts out his hand. I clasp it. Inside me something cold and hard is splintering. As I look round the room at the ill-treated faces, a rush of emotion replaces my apathy. No longer one of them, I immediately want to help them.

Words fly from me. Joe's hands grip my arms. I don't know whom I love, but suddenly I know where I'm going. To Italy, right back where I started from. To the country I can't remember, the country where I was born of displaced parents who once hoped to see their children native-born citizens. There, perhaps, I shall one day re-enter the strange land of love, where tomorrow is not always a threatening word.

SIGH FOR A STRANGE LAND